The Story
of a
Brief Marriage

The Story
of a
Brief Marriage

ANUK ARUDPRAGASAM

FLATIRON
BOOKS
NEW YORK

THE STORY OF A BRIEF MARRIAGE. Copyright © 2016 by Anuk Arudpragasam. All rights reserved. Printed in the United States of America. For information, address Flatiron Books, 175 Fifth Avenue, New York, N.Y. 10010.

www.flatironbooks.com

Designed by Kathryn Parise

The Library of Congress Cataloging-in-Publication Data is available upon request.

ISBN 978-1-250-07240-5 (hardcover)
ISBN 978-1-250-07475-1 (e-book)

Our books may be purchased in bulk for promotional, educational, or business use. Please contact your local bookseller or the Macmillan Corporate and Premium Sales Department at 1-800-221-7945, extension 5442, or by e-mail at MacmillanSpecialMarkets@macmillan.com.

First Edition: September 2016

10 9 8 7 6 5 4 3 2 1

The Story
of a
Brief Marriage

1

MOST CHILDREN HAVE two whole legs and two whole arms but this little six-year-old that Dinesh was carrying had already lost one leg, the right one from the lower thigh down, and was now about to lose his right arm. Shrapnel had dissolved his hand and forearm into a soft, formless mass, spilling to the ground from some parts, congealing in others, and charred everywhere else. Three of the fingers had been fully detached, where they were now it was impossible to tell, and the two remaining still, the index finger and thumb, were dangling from the hand by very slender threads. They swayed uncertainly in the air, tapping each other quietly, till arriving at last in the operating area Dinesh knelt to the ground, and laid the boy out carefully on an empty tarpaulin. His chest, it seemed, was hardly moving. His eyes were closed, and his face was calm, unknowing. That he was not in the best of conditions there could be no doubt, but all that mattered for the time being was that the boy was safe. Soon the doctor would arrive and the operation would be done, and in no time at all the arm would be as nicely healed as the already amputated thigh. Dinesh turned towards this thigh and studied the smooth, strangely well-rounded stump. According to the boy's sister the injury had come from a land mine explosion four months before, the same accident that killed their parents also. The amputation had been done at a nearby hospital, one of the few still functioning at the time, and there was hardly any scarring on the hairless skin, even the stitch marks were difficult to find. Dinesh had seen dozens of amputees with similar stumps in the last months, in different states of recovery depending on how much time had elapsed since each operation, but he was still somehow unable to believe in the reality of all the truncated limbs. They seemed, in some way, fake, or illusory. To dispel this thought of course he only needed to reach out now and touch the one in front of him, to learn once and for all if the skin around the stump was as smooth as it seemed or actually coarse, if the hardness of bone could be felt underneath, or if true to appearance the thing had the softness of spoiled fruit, but whether for fear of waking the child or something else, Dinesh did not move. He simply sat there with his face inches from the stump, completely still.

When the doctor arrived with one of the nurses close behind he knelt down next to the tarpaulin without a word and studied the mangled forearm. There were no surgical instruments in the clinic, no anesthetics, neither general nor local, no painkillers or antibiotics, but from the look on the doctor's face it was clear that there was no choice but to go on. He motioned for the nurse to hold down the boy's left arm and leg, for Dinesh to hold down the head and right shoulder. He raised up the kitchen knife they'd been using for amputations, checked to make sure it was properly clean, and then, nodding at his two assistants, placed its sharp point just below the right elbow. Dinesh readied himself. The doctor pressed down, the point pierced, and the boy, who had remained until then in a state of deep, silent sleep, came to life. His eyes opened, the veins along his neck and temples dilated, and he let out a tender shriek that continued without pause as the doctor, who had started slowly in the hope the boy would remain unconscious during the operation, sawed now firmly through the flesh, without hesitation. Blood trickled onto the tarpaulin and spilled out onto the soil. Dinesh cradled the boy's little head in his lap, softly caressed his scalp. Whether it was a good thing or bad that he was losing his right arm and not his left, it was hard to tell. Having only a left arm and a left leg would not help the boy's balance no doubt, but all things considered he might have been worse off with a right arm and a left leg, or a left arm and a right leg, for surely, if you thought about it, those combinations were less evenly weighted. Of course if his two good limbs had been on opposite sides the boy would have been able to use a crutch for walking, for then the crutch could have been held by his good arm, and could therefore have replaced the bad leg. In the end though it depended on what mode of transport the boy would have access to once healed, wheelchair, crutches, or just his single leg, and so whether or not he'd gotten lucky it was probably, at that point, premature to say.

The doctor continued cutting through the flesh, not with quick efficient strokes but with a jagged, sawlike motion. His face remained impassive, even as the knife began to grate against the bone, as if the eyes that looked on at the scene belonged to a different person from the hands that did the cutting. How the doctor kept going on this way, day after day, Dinesh had no idea. It was well known that as the front lines shifted east he had chosen to stay behind in the territory of his own volition, to help those trapped inside instead of moving to the safety of government-held areas. He'd moved from one hospital to another as they continued to be destroyed by the shelling, and when at last the divisional hospital he'd been working at in the camp had been shelled the previous week he'd decided, together with a small number of medical staff there, to convert the abandoned school building nearby into a makeshift clinic, hoping it would be inconspicuous enough to treat injured civilians in safety. They ran the clinic according to a kind of assembly line method: volunteers would first carry the injured to the operating area, where the nurses would clean their wounds, prepare each one so they were as ready as possible for their operation, then the doctor would come, perform the surgery, and move on immediately to the next person, leaving the nurses to stitch up the wounds and do the bandaging, unless a child was involved in which case the doctor insisted on doing everything himself. The injured person would then be moved to the area in front of the clinic, and accompanied there by relations and checked upon every so often by the nurses they either improved and were soon able to leave of their own accord, or died and had to be taken away by volunteers for burial. From morning to night each day the doctor moved in this way from patient to patient, showing no emotion whatsoever as he performed his operations, never wearying and hardly ever resting except when twice daily he stopped to eat, and then for a few hours each night when he tried to sleep. He was a great man Dinesh knew, deserving of endless praise, though looking at his face now it was impossible to tell what had allowed him to continue like this, and whether he was still in possession of any feelings.

The damp sound of the knife through flesh gave way to the scrape of its teeth against the tarpaulin, and at last the cutting stopped. The child's head was limp on Dinesh's lap, his face again unknowing.

The doctor lifted up what remained of the arm, which terminated now just past the elbow, and used a piece of cloth to absorb the blood still dripping. He dabbed the wound with another cloth, this one boiled in water and soaked in iodine, carefully sutured it shut with the thin flaps of excess skin, then dressed it neatly with one of their last bandages. When everything was done the doctor bore the boy up in his arms and went away with the nurse in search of a quiet place for him to rest. Dinesh, on whom the job of disposal fell, sat staring at the bloody little hand and forearm, wondering what he should do. There were plenty of other naked body parts scattered around the camp of course, fingers and toes, elbows and thighs, so many that nobody would say a thing if he just left the arm under a bush or beside a tree. But while those body parts were anonymous this one had an owner, which meant, he felt, that it had to be disposed of properly. He could bury it perhaps, or burn it, but he was apprehensive of touching it. Not because of the blood, for the child's blood had already stained his sarong and his hands, but because he didn't want to feel the softness of freshly amputated flesh between his fingers, the warmth of a limb just recently alive. He would much rather just wait till the blood had drained and the flesh had hardened, when picking the severed arm up would be more like picking up a stick or small branch, not much more perhaps but more so all the same. He was mulling over the issue when a girl with very thin ankles and long, broad feet came walking towards where he sat, her arms wrapped tightly around her chest and her fingers clutching the sides of her dress. She was the boy's older sister, his only living relative, coming from outside the clinic where she had been made to wait during the operation. Without a word to Dinesh or even a glance, no longer crying but her eyes still swollen and wet, she knelt down in front of the bloody tarpaulin and spread out a torn square of sari fabric over where her brother had just been lying. Picking up the remains carefully, so the hand didn't fall away from the forearm and the fingers didn't fall away from the hand, she placed them delicately on one edge of the cloth. She began very gently to roll the flesh up in the fabric, veiling it reverently in several soft layers as though it was a piece of supple gold jewelry, or something perishable that must be preserved for a long journey, and when it was wrapped so fully that nothing could be seen except the sari she stood up slowly, cradling the thing to her breast, and without saying a thing turned and walked away.

It was late afternoon and the day was overcast, devoid of movement. Shifting his weight onto his legs, Dinesh raised himself up. He stood still for a while till the dizziness from standing up dissipated, then fixing his eyes on the ground before him, began to walk east from the clinic. It had rained only a little the night before but the ochre soil between the tarpaulins had been stained maroon, glazed by a layer of smooth red slime. Wary of slipping in the mush or stepping on any of the splayed hands and feet, Dinesh took long, loping strides over the bodies, making sure with each step to set his front foot down properly before raising his back foot up from the ground. He felt slightly bad for leaving, but the urgent operations had more or less been finished, and for the time being at least there wasn't much work to be done. All day since the shelling he had been helping out around the clinic, the cries of the wounded and grieving flooding every space between his ears, and all he wanted now was a quiet place in which to sit, rest, and think, somewhere he could contemplate in peace the proposal he had received earlier that morning. He had been digging a

grave just north of the clinic when a tall, slightly stooped man he recognized from somewhere but was unable to place had grabbed him
by the hand, introduced himself as Somasundaram, and pulled him
away hurriedly to a corner. The slow and easy rhythm of his shoveling suddenly interrupted, Dinesh had done his best to come out of his
daze and make sense of what was happening. He had seen him working in the clinic the day before, the man was saying, and it was obvious he was a good boy, that he'd had some education, that he was
responsible, and of the right age. Ganga, his daughter, his only child
after her brother had been killed two weeks before, was a good girl
too. She was pretty, and smart, and responsible, but most of all, most
importantly, she was a good girl. He looked at Dinesh as he said this,
his eyes yellow and his hair unkempt, a gray scruff all over his hag-
gard face and neck, then lowered his gaze to the ground. In truth he
didn't want to get her married, he only wanted to keep her safe and
close beside him, for now that the rest of his family was gone he could
hardly bear to lose her too. He hadn't given marriage even a moment's
thought till the day before, he said wiping a tear from his cheek with
a dirty thumb, but as soon as he'd seen Dinesh in the clinic he'd known
it was his responsibility, that it was something he had to do for the sake
of his daughter. He was an old man, he was going to die soon, and it
was his duty to find someone to take care of her once he'd gone. It
didn't matter whether their horoscopes were compatible, or what day
or time was most auspicious, for obviously it was impossible to follow
all the customs all the time. Dinesh had some education and he was a
good, responsible boy, he said looking up again, and that was all that
mattered. There was an Iyer in the camp who could perform the rites,
and if he said yes then the Iyer would get them married immediately.

   At first Dinesh had just looked back at Mr. Somasundaram blankly, not knowing how to respond. He wasn't quite sure he'd followed everything that had been said and didn't really have time to think on it in any case, for the pit he was digging needed to be finished as quickly as possible, in order to free up space in the clinic for all the new arrivals from the morning's shelling. Seeing his hesitation, Mr. Somasundaram added that there was no hurry, that it was important Dinesh spend some time thinking about his decision. The Iyer had been wounded the day before, it was true, but he was doing well so far, and as long as Dinesh said yes by the afternoon there was no reason the Iyer wouldn't be fit enough to get them married. Dinesh was silent a little longer, then indicated that he understood. He remained standing where he was for a while after Mr. Somasundaram had gone, then turned back to the grave in order to resume digging. He thrust his spade into the earth, leaned his meager weight into the handle, and lifted out the soil he had loosened, tried to fall back into the rhythm of the shoveling. In a way he shouldn't really have been surprised by what had happened, of course, for it was obvious why Mr. Somasundaram was trying to marry his daughter, if not to him in particular then to any male of marriageable age he could find. Parents had been trying desperately to get their children married in the past two years, their daughters especially, hoping that once married they'd be less likely conscripted into the movement. By this point the married were just as likely to be recruited for the fighting as the unmarried it was true, but many continued trying to marry their daughters even so, believing that if they ended up in the hands of the government the girls that were married were less likely to be defiled, more likely to be passed over by the soldiers for other spoils. Why the proposal had been made was obvious, therefore, though what exactly it meant for him, and how he should respond to it, Dinesh found much more difficult to say. He should probably have made an effort to think about it sooner, to con-centrate his mind on the issue while he was still digging, but perhaps because the work before him was too distracting, or because he didn't yet know how to approach the matter, or because it was pleasing in some way to postpone dealing with it, he'd resigned himself to wait-ing until the grave was finished. As soon as the digging was over though he'd been told to begin moving bodies to the grave from the clinic, and then to help carry the injured to the clinic from the camp. In the midst of all the chaos and screaming he'd stopped thinking about the proposal completely and now, having finally been released from his duties, he found his initial lack of comprehension replaced by a quiet, sweeping astonishment. It was as though he'd been moving around, all this time, in a heavy fog, doing whatever he needed to do mindlessly, refusing to register the world outside him, and refusing to let it have any effect on him, so that having been caught off guard by the unexpected proposal, forced to wake up suddenly after how many months of being like this he didn't know, he was seeing his situation for the very first time now, keenly aware of the multitudes of people around him, and of himself as he navigated uncertainly through the camp.

They had accrued there, many tens of thousands of them, over a period of a few weeks. A few of them had been displaced recently from nearby villages, but most of them were refugees from villages to the north, south and west who had abandoned their homes long before and been on the move for many months, some, like Dinesh, for almost a year. Each time they set up camp somewhere they had hoped it would be the last time before the movement finally pushed back the govern-ment, and each time they were forced again by the advancing shell-ing to pack up and move further east. Stopping and starting they had traveled like this across the breadth of the northern province, herded by the shelling into the increasingly small pocket of territory remaining in the northeast, till hearing about the still-functioning divisional hospital and the camp that had started to form around it, assured by the movement that the area was safe and that the army would never be able to take it, they had come in desperation at last to the camp, followed by more and more every day, each party adding to the settlement of tents around the hospital like a massive temple that was being erected around a small, golden shrine. The first shells had fallen on the camp only two weeks earlier, on the hospital just the week before, and every day since then the shelling had gotten heavier and more sustained. Each bout dotted the densely populated area with dozens of circles of scorched black earth, most of which remained empty for only a while before being taken over by new tenants. Every part of the camp was bombed, even one of the school buildings that housed the makeshift clinic had been hit, despite its small size, and in the last few days probably a seventh or eighth of those living there had been killed. There was talk that the final assault on the area would be made in the next few days, that the divisional hospital would soon stop functioning, that even the doctor and his staff were making plans to abandon the clinic and set up further east, and in response some people had already begun to pack up and leave. A few were trying to cross over to the government side in the hope they would be taken in, though the fighting on the front lines was almost certainly too fierce to get through alive. The movement would shoot if they caught anyone escaping, and even if they made it to the other side, nobody could tell what the soldiers would do to them when they arrived. Most were planning to move further east instead, closer towards the coast and further away from the front lines, though the ones who wanted to stay behind claimed the shelling there was probably just as bad. There was no point moving further east just out of habit, they said, there was only a little bit of land left now, in less than two kilometers they would reach the sea and there would be nowhere left to go. A story had circulated about a week before about a group of twenty-five or thirty who had taken an abandoned fishing boat out in the hope of making it somehow to India. Two days later the boat had washed back up on shore, carrying inside it the bodies of a few adults and several children, riddled with bullets, pale blue and bloated. The best option therefore was just to stay in the camp till the fighting ended, they argued, to stay put in the dugouts whenever the shells fell and hope they would survive unscathed till the end.

That things would work out this way Dinesh was, needless to say, a little skeptical. He didn't have conclusive evidence that he would die rather than survive, but perhaps because in such conditions it was easier to believe something than to remain unsure, he felt himself tending towards the former possibility. The fighting showed no signs of abating, and it was only a matter of time he felt before he would either be killed in the shelling, or conscripted and then killed in the fighting. And if that was indeed the case, if in fact he had only a few days or weeks left to his credit, a month at most if he was lucky, his guiding consideration in deciding what to do must be to make use of the time remaining as best he could, in which case perhaps it made sense for him to get married. Perhaps it would be good for him to spend the time he had left in the company of another human being. In spite of having been surrounded for most of the past year by countless numbers of people, he couldn't tell when the last time was that he'd really felt connected to somebody else. He couldn't even remember what it was like to spend time with another person, to simply be in someone else's company, and perhaps it would be worthwhile to do so if he could. Didn't dying in the end mean being separated from other humans, after all, from the sea of human gaits, gestures, noises, and gazes in which for so many years one had floated, didn't it mean abandoning the possibility of connecting with another human that being among others always afforded? Unless, on the other hand, dying meant being separated from oneself above all, being separated from all the intimate personal details that had come to constitute one's life. If that was the case then surely he should try instead to be alone, should spend his remaining time committing to memory the shape of his hands and feet, the texture of his hair, fingernails and teeth, appreciating for a last time the sound of his own breathing, the sensation of his chest expanding and contracting. What dying meant there was no way he could really know of course, it was a subject he was not in a position to think about clearly. It depended probably on what living meant, and though he had been alive for some time it was difficult to remember whether it had meant being together with other humans, or being alone with himself above all.

Dinesh noticed that the ground was no longer passing by beneath him. He had come to a stop apparently, though how long he'd been standing there motionless he didn't know. From the dusty barrenness of the area he could tell he was near the northeastern end of the camp, quite far now from the clinic. Spread out around him and bounded in the distance by dusty brush and tired, drooping trees were a few white tents, the most recent additions to the camp, propped up by sticks no more than three or four feet high. The area around them was scattered with things, with bags, bundles, pots, pans, and cycles, and lying or crouching on the ground beside them were people in groups of three and four, some sleeping, others merely waiting, as far as he could see not a single one of them speaking. Passing a woman who was sitting by herself and eating sand compulsively from the ground—handful after handful, not chewing, since sand can't be chewed, but mixing the sand with saliva and then simply swallowing—Dinesh walked towards a thin, leafless tree. He fell wearily against its base, let the bark press pleasantly against his back, and stretched out his legs so that the muscles in his thighs, exhausted from all the digging, could finally relax. Leaning forward he buried his face between his hands. He hadn't slept at all that night, hardly at all that whole week. There was a throbbing deep in the back of his head and his eyes were heavy, as if lead had accumulated along the bottom of his eyelids, stretching them out so much that soon they would become translucent. He let them close and massaged his eyelids thickly with his thumbs, listened to the blood pulse softly through the slender sieves of skin, beating heavily upon his tired eyes. It wasn't that he hadn't tried to go to bed, but no matter how tired he was and how much he tried, he could never sleep very long or fully. It was a light sleep he always had, superficial and easily interrupted. Perhaps it had something to do with the fact that it was difficult to sleep in an unfamiliar place, as when taking a new bus or train route you would always be slightly afraid that something bad would happen if you dozed off, that your bag might be stolen or that you might miss your stop. Dinesh had been in the camp for almost three weeks though, and if he didn't feel at home there he was in any case no longer a complete stranger, the little space he had made for himself in the jungle just northeast of the clinic was quiet and comfortable, a place he could rest whenever he liked as if in the safety of his own room. He would go there each night to lie down, but as soon as he closed his eyes and began drifting towards sleep, his consciousness rocking softly back and forth in the direction of dream, he would feel a hesitation or foreboding growing suddenly inside him. It was as if in falling asleep he was exposing himself to a danger that could only be avoided by staying awake, as though upon fully losing awareness the ground would give way beneath him and he would drop backwards through the darkness towards an impact he did not want to face.

There was, always, before the shelling, for the slenderest moment before the earth began shaking, a faraway whispering, as of air hurtling at high speed through a thin tube, a whooshing, which turned, indiscernibly, into a whistling. This whistling lasted for a while, and then, no matter where you stood, there was a tremulous vibration, the trembling of the earth underfoot, followed by a blast of hot air against the skin, and then finally the deafening explosion. It was a loud, unbearably loud explosion, followed immediately by others, so loud that as soon as the first one came the rest could no longer be heard. They could be registered only as the pervasive absence of sound, as a series of voids or vacuums in the sound sphere so great that not even the sound of thinking could be heard. The world became mute, like a silent film, and as a result the bombing often brought about in Dinesh a sense of calm. He wouldn't jump up or rush to shelter but would first stand still and take a deep breath, look around with amazement and also slight confusion, as though the thread that had guided his movements in the quiet before the shelling had suddenly been cut. He would try to gather his bearings, and would only then begin walking, slowly, and calmly, not to any of the dugouts that had been built throughout the camp but towards the stretch of jungle that separated the camp's northeast boundary from the coast. Wandering around one day he had found a small wooden fishing boat that someone had hauled inland and turned over, the owner probably, in the hope that it would be safer there than on the beach. Moss had begun to spread over its painted surface but the name, Sahotharaa, was still visible, upside down near the front. The boat's rim curved upwards towards the bow and stern, and he found that he could squeeze in through the middle section into its shelter, dark and cool and private. The air was slightly stale but the boat was long and there was room inside to stretch out, even to sleep, though for some reason Dinesh couldn't lie flat while the bombs fell. Instead he sat upright, hunched forward to avoid the low ceiling, legs bent in front of him and arms drawn around his knees. He would sit there for what seemed like hours staring at the ground before him, the wood creaking with each new explosion, gusts of hot air rushing in and then receding through the gaps between boat and ground, slackening his body instead of tightening it so he could feel himself tremble as the earth shook. He felt at such times always strangely disembodied, as though observing himself from the outside, watching as his two hands clasped each other tightly and as his fingers intertwined of their own accord. He listened passively as his chest expanded and contracted, as air went in and out of his mouth, and he stayed that way, breathing in and out, long after the shelling had stopped.

Not everyone reacted this way naturally and neither did Dinesh in the beginning, when his mother was alive still and he was less resigned to all that was happening around him. In the beginning he was inseparable from the general clambering, from the shouting and screaming and the frantic attempts to find friends and relatives before the shelling grew so fierce that everyone had to stop moving. Using wooden boards and bricks from nearby buildings and working together, people in the camp had managed to construct hundreds of dugouts in which to hide during the bombings, some of them as deep as six feet, though most of them were only about four feet deep and just large enough for nine or ten people to sit crouching with their bodies tightly packed together. Coconut and palmyra leaves were kept beside the openings, sheets of corrugated steel if they were lucky, and when it was time to get under they would climb down and draw these covers over their heads. The dugouts didn't provide protection if a shell landed in the immediate vicinity, and though they did help against the shrapnel, by far the greatest source of injury and death, the most significant benefit they gave their occupants was the comfort of being surrounded by four close walls, a floor, and a ceiling, like ostriches that, in times of great danger, choose not to run away but rather to dig into the earth and bury their heads inside, regardless of how exposed their bodies are. The ground beneath them reverberating with the force of each explosion, the clay soil crumbling bit by bit from the earthen walls, they would sit in the darkness of these dugouts with their bodies tensely still while inside their heads their thoughts raced like gas particles in a heated container, estimating where each shell had fallen relative to their location, speculating whether known people might have been hurt in a particular explosion, predicting where subsequent shells would fall based on various patterns, and revising their models when mistaken, comforted, all the while, only by the smallness of the space and the breathing, tight or loose, fast or slow, of the others squeezed in around them.

If they learned somehow that someone they knew was killed in the bombing outside, the women would begin to hit themselves and scream. They beat their heads against the dugout walls and pulled wildly at their hair till it tore from the roots, so that at the end of each spell of shelling many of the dugouts were full of clumps of long, dirty hair. If a relative was hurt out in the open they would run out from their shelters screaming and crying, and raising their pleading faces to the sky they would try to drag the wounded body back to safety, hauling it by a shirt or trouser leg, by a hand or foot or even a few strands of hair, even if it became clear the person had died. The men on the other hand were generally quieter, sometimes almost impassive. Perhaps a single tear streaming mutely down their faces, slowly and wordlessly they would walk out to the dead bodies of their kinsmen and kneel down in front of them, even as the ground shook and shells exploded around them. They sat down beside the bodies of their beloveds and sobbed in silence, rocking back and forth, oblivious to everything happening around them. Lovingly they stroked the body's face and chest. Gently they kneaded the eyelids, massaged the arms and kissed the hands. Bending down they buried their faces in the dead person's neck and inhaled deeply, as though to commit to memory the person's distinctive smell. Whereas the women reminded Dinesh of the severed tails of geckos, which thrash about for a long time after the body that has supported them for so long has gone, bravely refusing to give up hope even after the source of all life and meaning has been destroyed, the men reminded him of the frogs he'd learned about long ago in school, whose spinal cords were cut by scientists to study the difference between the higher and lower brains. Unlike the frogs you saw in ponds and puddles, whose wet skin was always expanding and contracting and whose deep, satisfied voices were always rising and falling, the embodiment of organic flourishing, these mutilated frogs were completely still and silent, oblivious to all stimuli, passive even when poked or prodded. Whether they were hungry or thirsty, calm or scared, it was impossible to tell for the only

movement they made was when they were pushed over, in response
to which they merely righted themselves and resumed their blankness, a blankness they kept till they died.

When the shelling was over a deep silence pervaded the camp.
That it was over always took a while to dawn, for all had their eyes
closed, their hands clasped over their ears, and their faces pressed tight
to the earth. Nobody in the camp could tell with certainty when the
loud silence of the bombing was replaced by the soft silence of the stillness, and it was always better safe than sorry anyway, for sometimes
the barrage of shelling would cease for ten or fifteen minutes only to
suddenly start up again, as if to trick them into thinking that everything was over so they would come out into the open to help the injured. Only much later, once their senses had finally returned, when
they began to smell the burned flesh and hear the crying of the
wounded, could any of them be sure the bombing was over. Even then
most remained motionless where they were, their features expressionless. A small number, a few more every time, would have distorted,
inhuman smiles twisted across their faces. They rubbed the fabrics of
their sarongs and dresses, rolled bits of earth around in their hands
and laughed strangely, whispered to themselves. Dinesh had once seen
a man with an amputated arm wandering around after the shelling as
if in search of his missing body part; he picked up the different fore-
arms he found on the ground and tried each one on like he was shopping for new clothes, pursing his lips with dissatisfaction at each
mismatch of size or complexion. Those who were able to do so collected themselves and began the work of tending to the wounded and
gathering together the dead. There wasn't enough kerosene to burn
all the bodies and so instead they simply buried them, wrapping each
body in swathes of cloth or tarpaulin and then depositing them in pits

dug at sites near the edges of the camp, unless a shell had fallen on a dugout in which case the dugout was simply filled back up with earth. In the last few days the work that digging graves required had become too great and most of the corpses that weren't claimed by relatives were just covered up with tarpaulin sheets or leaves, sometimes even left uncovered in the same place they'd been found. Many of the bodies weren't fully whole anyway, and somehow it seemed more appropriate to let them be as they were than to bury only the largest pieces they could find.

A strange feeling always came over Dinesh as he wandered around in the silence after the bombing. Even if he had some specific task to do, if he was digging a grave for the dead, or helping transport the wounded to the hospital or clinic, still he felt he didn't quite know what he was doing or where he was going. For a long time he would wander around the burned and disturbed camp lost, disoriented, like a leaf detached from its tree and blown haphazardly over barren land, without link to any living thing. It was similar perhaps to the feeling he used to have when he was left alone at home as a young child, worrying at first that his mother and father had taken too long returning and then believing they had somehow died, crying with the certainty of being left alone for the rest of his life in a vast, unknown world. It was similar to this feeling but different, for how could he be expected to feel the loss of things he could no longer even remember? He'd been isolated from his home, family, friends, and possessions so long that such a separation could no longer feel painful or even unusual. It was more than just disconnection from once familiar people and things that he felt, more than just a sense of being isolated; above all it was the disintegration of his body that came to mind at such times, the disintegration of his hair, his teeth, his skin. His nails no longer growing, his skin no longer sweating. He sensed acutely the fact that soon his body would begin breaking down, sensed in fact that the process of becoming permanently separate from it had already begun. All his life he had used his hands and feet, his fingers and toes, and knowing that soon he'd no longer be able to rely on them made him feel abandoned suddenly and alone, as when at a train station or the seaside, about to emigrate far away, you must say good-bye to the friends and family you thought would be present all through your life. Similarly too he felt when he thought about the hair that grew all over his body, the hair on his head, the curly hair of his calves, thighs, and groin, the fine golden-black hair of his arms, and so too with the hair of his eyelashes and eyebrows. All his life he'd been indifferent to these things but it was impossible now to feel this way, for they had been there with him through everything, through his whole life, and were now about to leave for good. His eyes and ears, his knuckles and knees, and also the organs inside him, which he'd never seen nor thought to thank but which had worked tirelessly for him all his life, selflessly. What it would be like to be separated from all these things he did not know, he could not envision, but the more he dwelled on it the more he understood that it was not so much fear of being separated that he felt as sadness at the idea of parting.

Dinesh opened his eyes onto the brightness of the world before him. He stretched his arms out and shuffled further back up against the tree he was leaning on. He felt an urge, suddenly, to empty his bowels. Not so much a bodily urge, for he'd hardly eaten anything in the last few days, hardly enough for there to be any excess, but more of a psychological urge, an urge he might nevertheless satisfy physically, he felt, since after all it was only a matter of pushing hard enough. The nearest place he could go was the outhouse not far from the clinic, but in addition to shit it was filled with blood and vomit, on the walls and all over the ground, and he wouldn't be able to take his time there. He wanted somewhere quiet, somewhere comfortable, somewhere he could take his time. There was a secluded section of coastline he could use, though there was some danger now in venturing too far out from the camp, especially towards the coast, where the movement ran patrols and there was a chance he could be caught and recruited. There was also the fact of its being too wide and exposed an area, too open a place for the privacy needed for a long and peaceful shit. He wanted to take it slow, to be alone somewhere he could listen in comfort to the sound of his bowels for a last time, listen for clues as to his origin and destination. The beach was quiet but it was too open, and he would feel watched by some distant eye, not fully at ease. The only alternative however was the jungle that bounded the camp to the north and east, and in the daytime especially other camp residents would be coming and going there, wanting to relieve themselves likewise. He had grown used to shitting in view of other people of course, or at least to shitting with the possibility of others walking by, and he could do that if the situation demanded but it meant he wouldn't be able to take his time. The jungle was full of undergrowth too and he would have to shit while crouching on the uneven ground. The earth there would be wet, or moist at least, the bark and leaves also, whereas he wanted to be somewhere dry. Maybe he would go to the seaside then, where there would also be water with which he could wash. He would find a quiet spot where he could feel alone and unwatched, where he'd be able to hear the sound of waves washing over the sand, of birds calling in the distance through the salty air.

Dinesh struggled to lift himself up from his place against the tree, but as soon as he was on his feet his body began to move as though it

knew where to go of its own accord. He floated through the desolation of the camp towards its northern boundary, past the last remaining
tents and the silent groups of two and three, into the dusty, browning
brush. Effortlessly his feet negotiated the tangle of roots and shrubs,
skirted the occasional body parts and little mounds of shit, leaving
him free to watch as the brush gave way to denser vegetation and
trees, to finely veined leaves and gray and brown barks. To some degree it was foolish of him to be going to the beach he knew, where
he could be spotted from many miles away if he were not careful. He
was of fighting age after all, of good height although a little thin. If
he was seen by army gunboats there was no doubt he would be shot
at, and if he was seen by the movement's patrols he'd be conscripted,
and probably beaten too for having avoided recruitment so long. How
in fact he'd managed to escape till then it was difficult to say, for there
were hardly any boys his age left now in the camp. He'd taken care
not to use crowded routes during the displacements naturally, and to
avoid the areas where other civilians set up their tents. Now that the
retreating had come to an end he stayed hidden in the jungle most of
the day, and if he went to the camp it was only in the hours immediately after the shelling, when the disarray was too great for anyone to
notice him. He never let himself hang around too long but in truth
he'd taken his chances plenty of times, and it could only have been by
luck that he hadn't yet been seen. In a sense he probably wouldn't have
cared that much earlier, if he actually had been recruited, since between the two ways of dying there hadn't seemed very much to choose,
though thinking on the issue now, it was clear that his attitude had
changed. Apart from the question of marriage it suddenly seemed
obvious that he was better off not conscripted, for compared to the
cadres, who spent every waking moment defending the movement's

remaining land, even civilians had some peace of mind. As a civilian at least he had time to think, whereas as a cadre he would have to fight on the front lines, his ears full of the deafening pounding of guns, right until he was killed. All things considered, therefore, it was best he avoid being seen. Never mind his plan about shitting, he told himself as he continued making his way through the jungle, if there was any sign of trouble he would turn back immediately and run. Dinesh noticed that the vegetation around him was becoming drier and less dense, the soil lighter and a little sandier. Looking up he realized that he could make out the horizon ahead, then soon after, beyond the short bushes and a few solitary coconut trees, the sea. He took off his slippers and held them in his hands, felt the fine grains of sand bristling under the arches of his feet and between his toes. From behind the cover of a tree he looked cautiously from left to right and from right to left, and then walked, for the first time in how long he could not say, onto the beach.

It was late January or early February but the water was calm, extending endlessly from the sand like an untarnished blue sheet of steel, devoid of waveforms and fishing boats. Dinesh's feet sank into the soft white sand, and his thin, tired calves strained with each step to lift up his body, which was heavy now, no longer light or ghostlike. He went down to where the beach sloped gently towards the sea, where land and water met and the moist white sand was smooth and polished, easy to walk upon. Half circles of water lapped softly at his feet. A last little bit of sun was visible through the knot of heavy clouds, a funnel of white light that fell through the sky, illuminating a silver square of sea far across the horizon. Soon the sun would sink and the sky would darken Dinesh knew; he had to make use of his time as best he could. He walked north along the soft wet sand to where the coast

melted into the outlying dunes of a kind of desert from further inland. The beach rose gently from the sea for a few feet and then the
sand began to collect in quiet swellings, rising and falling, forming
large hills of sparkling white sea sand that became indistinguishable
from the dunes. Dinesh trudged towards a section of the coastline that
was enclosed by a circle of these hills, forming a kind of private, isolated beach. With some effort he climbed up onto one of them, looked
around to make sure the area was deserted, then wearily let himself
jog back down to the enclosed area of beach, not far from the water.
The sand wasn't fully wet but was moist enough still to form clumps,
and kneeling down he began to dig a small pit in the sand, carefully
scooping out a hemisphere of six-inch radius. Not far away, in the
camp and scattered beyond, there were hundreds of rotting bodies,
their parts strewn across the ground, men, women, and children with
festering wounds, mosquitoes buzzing over the living and flies over
the dead, but in spite of this freely spilling blood and flesh it was still
important, Dinesh felt, that his excreta be properly disposed of. It was
vital he dig a good hole in which to bury his shit, he felt, for the offering
he was making to the earth would be void if not properly presented.

Dinesh set down his slippers on the sand. He took off his shirt, laid
it out neatly upon the slippers, untied his sarong and placed it carefully
over the shirt. He stood there in silence, unclothed upon the still-
warm evening sand, staring up at the waveless blue body of water that
stretched out in front of him. There was nobody nearby but all the same
he was nervous to be there, entirely unclothed, about to assume so
vulnerable a position. There weren't many skirmishes at this time of
day but it was impossible of course to say with certainty. Even if there
was no danger of fighting there was still a chance an army gunboat
might pass by, and if one did there was little doubt that he would be

shot at. Dinesh looked out over the water for a while, watching as little ripples disturbed the surface briefly and then disappeared as gentle gusts of wind blew by and then died. He bent his legs slowly, then crouched down with his bottom over the pit. Leaning all his weight onto the balls of his feet and adjusting his body so he was comfortable, he got himself ready, then hesitated slightly. As defenseless as he already was in that position, there was something even more vulnerable about actually tightening his insides and trying to push. Once he started though the discomfort would most probably go away he knew, and so looking up at the funnel of light falling over the sea he strained, once, and then again. It felt strange to strain so hard while looking over the endless sky and the endless sea, to crouch down over his little pit in full view of the earth's enormous face. Averting his gaze from the horizon, he concentrated instead on the clothes laid out neatly next to where he crouched, and strained again. He tightened the muscles deep and low inside his body and pushed till he could feel his bowels moving within, shifting and sliding, the whole of his thin, weak body struggling to send out one final offering into the world. It was hard to excrete any bodily waste when he'd hardly eaten in two days and had had nothing but soggy rice for days before that, but his nervousness at being seen slowly began to leave him, and he tried to relax, to take his time. He built up a strong exertion inside his bowels and then strained, hard, repeated this cycle till finally he felt a light, tingling wetness in his backside. Encouraged, he relaxed, then strained, relaxed, and strained, did his best to eke out from his body as much as possible. He had hoped to fill the pit at least halfway but realized now that there was no chance, the delicate brown substance he was squeezing out would not even cover its floor. He gave one last strain, then moved aside and brought his face down to the pit to examine his production.

It was soft and airy, a creamy beige froth over a watery brown liquid, like the foam the sea sometimes deposits on the shore. It was a paltry offering no doubt, but it had come from him at least. It smelled familiar, at least. It was not rich and heavy and rounded, but he had made it himself, with his thin, weak body, and the earth, he knew, would be grateful.

Slowly he began to refill the pit. He filled his fists with sand and let the sand trickle down from between his fingers, so it sprinkled evenly upon the shit. When the foam's surface was entirely covered he filled the rest of the pit with a few large handfuls, then smoothed over its surface so its location on the beach couldn't be discovered merely by examination. He lay down prostrate beside it so that his elbows and knees pressed against the sand, so that the sand tingled his naked limbs. Closing his eyes he listened to the waves as they washed gently across the coast, to the sound of the water rolling and unrolling itself out over the shore. He felt his chest expand and contract, felt the air enter him and leave, and lowering his head down Dinesh let himself fill up with the lightly sulfurous odor that still emanated from inside the covered pit, all that was left of his final shit. With his index and middle fingers he caressed the sand in front of him, traced light lines over the surface of the generous earth that for so many years had provided him with space on which to sleep and stand. He dug his hand deep inside the sand and squeezed hard, so he could feel the grainy edges sharp against his skin, brought a handful to his face and inhaled, to commit to memory that strange dry smell of moist salt and dust that he would probably not smell again. He brought his face close to the warm sand over the pit once more and breathed in, but already he was unable to smell the faint presence of his shit.

Dinesh stood up, walked to the water, and washed himself, splashed the cool water over his legs and bottom. The water was clean, clear, and he felt the urge suddenly to wash himself, to clean his body of the blood and grime he had carried on his skin for so many weeks. The water was inviting but he should probably wait he knew, for he had spent enough time already on the beach and there was no point pushing his luck. He could bathe later in one of the wells around the camp, if he wanted, the water there would be less salty and he might even be able to find soap. He straightened out his naked body, and looked out over the still and silent surface of the sea, no longer illuminated now by the column of light. The clouds, backlit weakly in places by the sun, had thickened over, and the horizon as a whole had darkened. Without warning, the sky lit up in silvery incandescence. A great bellow sounded from down the coast and Dinesh flinched, ducked down into the water. He stayed squat with his hands over his head, his eyes shut, his heart pounding. There was a tense, heavy silence, followed, after a moment, by a light pattering, as of tiny glass beads being poured over the surface of the earth. As he opened his eyes cautiously Dinesh felt weightless spots of moisture on his skin, and raising his head he saw rain sweeping across the great and silent sea, falling across the horizon, thinly at first like fine spray, then more heavily. They fell like pins from the sky, gathering speed as they fell, coalescing as they dropped down through the atmosphere, each one collecting mass and momentum as it joined others on its journey, becoming fuller and denser till they fell to the earth finally and disintegrated upon its solid and liquid surfaces. The waveless surface of the sea was perforated by a thousand tiny pellets and then, just as softly, the rain ceased.

2

THERE WAS A PLEASANT lightness in his insides as Dinesh made his way back through the vegetation, a sense of being unencumbered that he tried to preserve by moving slowly and deliberately, with as few abrupt movements as possible. His thoughts had shifted, for the first time since the proposal, in the direction of Mr. Somasundaram's daughter, as though only now was he realizing that being married meant spending the rest of your life with one particular person, and that a marriage could be good or bad depending on the nature of that person. They had never actually spoken to each other but he remembered having seen Ganga around the clinic a few times before, tall, gaunt, and silent, her gaze always lowered to the ground. The very first time he'd seen her, probably the only reason he recognized her subsequently at all, he had been walking through the camp after a period of short but intense shelling. He had come by a group of people who'd gathered around to watch something, and stopping to find out what was going on he had stood on his tiptoes and seen, in the center of the circle they formed, a girl alone on the ground beside two bodies. The girl was struggling to take in air, wheezing almost. Her upper body was reeling back and forth, her two long plaits of hair daintily pirouetting on her shoulders. A few feet behind her stood a man, Mr. Somasundaram, his eyes wide and unblinking, gazing at the two bodies as if at nothing of particular note. The others were looking just as much at him as at the girl, more so in fact, but it took a while for Dinesh to realize that this was because the bodies on the ground were his wife and son, and that the girl leaning over them was his daughter. Watching her as she raised her mother's limp hand to her face and pressed it against her cheek, repeated to herself in a quiet, quivering voice that it was by that same hand that she had been fed, smacked, and cleaned, Dinesh had done his best to understand what it must be like to lose a mother and brother simultaneously. A similar thing had happened to him earlier in the war but it was hard to tell exactly, for he was so long cut off from the feeling. On some level obviously it must have been upsetting. The girl must have been in some pain, for the shells that killed her two family members had exploded only two, two and a half hours before. But in addition if not in contrast to the pain in her contorted features, there was, Dinesh felt, beneath these contortions, something also strangely dignified in the girl's face, something solemn, almost strict in her expression. In her wet eyes and the way she pursed her lips between her moans the girl it seemed had already arrived at an understanding of her situation, at a kind of pained but meticulous acceptance of it. Her mother and brother had died, but the world wouldn't stop moving, she seemed to recognize. Afternoon would turn into evening, the shells would continue falling, and the sooner she resigned herself to what had happened and went on living the better. If for the time being she was letting her body wrap itself around the bodies of her mother and brother, if she was letting herself shiver, cry, or shudder, then it was not because she was ignorant of this fact but because she knew her body had to respond in certain ways to what had happened, because she understood that it would do what it needed to do, regardless of her, and that there was no point trying to stop it.

A few days later Dinesh saw Ganga working in the clinic for the first time, her face smooth as a soft stone, expressionless, and despite her gauntness, somehow gentle. It wasn't that she had forgotten or gotten over the deaths, for there were still little aftershocks in which she stopped whatever she was doing and for a moment seemed to tremble, almost flutter, but these waves passed by quickly and for the most part she seemed strangely calm, determined. She worked harder than most of the other volunteers, in spite of and almost spurred on by her exhaustion, and unlike most of them both male and female no matter what she had to see or do she never seemed to feel faint. When there wasn't any urgent work to be done she would wander round the clinic in search of ways to help the injured, she would clean their wounds and change their bandages, try to put them in touch with relatives from whom they'd been sundered, and all that together with the task of taking care of her father left her with hardly even a moment, Dinesh felt, to be still. Only a couple of times in the late evening, when all of the injured who could had managed to put aside their pain for a little while and get some sleep before the next shelling, had he ever seen her sitting quietly by herself in the camp, and even then she seemed restless. She would untie her hair, let it lie slack for a bit against the curve of her back, then draw it tightly back across her scalp, combing it so not a strand was left free over her forehead or ears. Holding it fast as fiercely as she could, she would tie it back up without letting up on the pressure, so that when she was done her hair was plastered almost perfectly to her head. She would sit looking slightly lost, her eyes large in the stark beauty of her face, stroking her hair continuously and feeling its tight pull against the skin of her temples and scalp till suddenly, as though detecting a loosening in the tension, she would let her hair out once more and begin anew the process of tying it, more tightly this time if possible than before.

Unlike his daughter Mr. Somasundaram didn't at first, for some reason, seem affected by the deaths. For several days he continued doing the work he'd been doing around the camp in the previous weeks, setting up tents for the new arrivals, procuring rice for those who couldn't afford it, and directing the building of dugouts and bunkers. He'd been the principal of a large girl's school somewhere Dinesh had heard, and that together with his height perhaps had led others in the camp to give him a kind of deference in practical matters. This deference was amplified probably by the fact that he was one of the few men in the camp who'd managed to keep his family alive and together till then, though in retrospect, of course, this had turned out to be due more to chance than to any wisdom or divine grace. Perhaps it was because he too had believed in this aura of being able to keep others safe that Mr. Somasundaram didn't respond at first when his wife and son died. Perhaps he simply hadn't prepared himself properly for the possibility. He couldn't have consciously expected the shelling to spare his family obviously—by the time they died he must have seen the fate of enough families to know the same would likely happen to them too, in the end—but perhaps it was similar to how, when playing sports, you could never really give up or resign yourself to losing right till the very end. Even if you knew you were going to lose, even if you had long given up trying, the fact of defeat always dawned on you newly and almost incredibly when the final whistle was blown or wicket taken, the warm shiver of recognition that you'd failed sank in only after the match was lost, once everything was over, sometimes only several hours later, and perhaps something similar had happened to Mr. Somasundaram, too. It was hard to say for sure obviously but in any case, for many days after the deaths of his wife and son, Mr. Somasundaram went on as though nothing particularly important had occurred in his life. Only later, as though the news recorded immediately by his nerve endings had needed time to be absorbed down through his skin, did he begin to show any sign of grief. He began to do less work around the camp. He rested more, and talked less. Day by day his various activities diminished till finally, more than two weeks after the deaths, he no longer did anything at all, simply sat by himself outside his tent, hardly moving, shaking his head or shrugging if anyone in the camp came to him hoping for advice or support.

Every afternoon and night, at slightly different times depending on the pattern of the day's shelling, Ganga would put the rice and dhal she cooked for her father on one of the plates they had brought from home, and set it down on the ground before him. Mr. Somasundaram would nod with his eyes closed, not even raising his head, and motion for her to leave him alone. Sometimes he ate a little without being prompted, but more often he just left the plate where it was. Sometimes, in a low, slow voice, loud enough to be heard but not for any emotion to be discerned, he said the rice was too dry or too wet, as though that was the sole reason he wouldn't eat. Ganga would nudge the plate closer towards him, frown slightly as if he were neglecting his duties, and insist he eat a little at least, for what would people say if they found out he was not eating? If he still refused she would try a different approach, she would sit down next to him with the plate between them and make it clear she wouldn't leave until it was empty, knowing her father preferred to be alone and hoping he would eat if only to be rid of her. Even if she became convinced her father could genuinely not bear the thought of eating Ganga would sit there trying to force the food upon him, as if in obedience no longer to her father's wishes but to some higher law, and it was only when she was certain her father would not give in that finally she gave up trying. She would look around uneasily, anger mingled with embarrassment on her face, perhaps also a little shame, then get up and take the food to one of the many people in the camp who were close to starving, taking care to explain that she had cooked too much rice rather than that her father was not hungry.

Dinesh had come to the area of the camp just east of the clinic, not far from where Mr. Somasundaram's tent was located, and for several minutes had been surveying the tents and people spread out before him. He was searching, he realized now with some surprise, for Ganga and her father. What exactly he was going to do he couldn't be sure until he was actually in front of them, until he actually heard himself saying yes or no to the proposal, but the fact was that he was trying to find them, and with more earnestness probably than if he were going to say no. How exactly it had happened and for what reasons if any he couldn't tell, but in some obscure region inside him the question of marriage had already been settled it seemed, independently, apparently, of him. Perhaps that was all there was to making a decision— waiting patiently as the various possibilities settled in the mind of their own accord—or perhaps, unknown to him, some part of him had in fact been actively thinking, for the decision made sense if he thought about it, in a way. If the proposal had come earlier in the fighting, when he had been with his mother still and when they were under the

impression that soon they would be returning home, his consider-
ations would probably have been different, but now his mother was gone,
and so too most of their relatives, most people from the village too.
Who was there to arrange a marriage for him now, and why should
he wait till later to get married anyway, as though somehow another
opportunity was going to come along? The fact was that soon he
would die, and saying yes would mean he could spend his last few days
with a person, with not just a person but with a girl, with a woman,
a wife. It was foolish to worry about whether he was giving up the
chance to spend time being with himself, for even if he spent the rest
of his brief life with Ganga it would still be his body that was next to
hers, and it would still be possible for him to be alone with himself
in her presence. What they would do together, he didn't know. How
husbands and wives spent their time he had no idea, but at the very
least he would be able to sit beside her, to eat beside her, and think beside her, do with her whatever it was that people in general did with
each other. He would be able to take care of her, put his arm around
her slender body and comfort her, bring her close to him and hug her
tight, make her feel secure, and she would be able to do the same for
him also. And who knew, maybe they could even make love to each
other. What it involved exactly and whether he was able he wasn't
quite sure, but it was what married couples did on their wedding night
or shortly thereafter he knew, and perhaps they could do the same
too, before they died.

Dinesh caught sight of Ganga at last sitting on the ground, partially obscured behind a tent. She was holding a child in her arms,
rocking it gently from side to side, staring straight through its face as
though at something underneath it. Dinesh watched her for a while
without moving, completely still save the heavy beating of his heart,

then advanced in her direction till he was standing right in front of her, looking down at her almost. She didn't look up immediately; her eyes shifted from the child's face to the human-shaped shadow suddenly cast on the ground before her, she studied it with curiosity, and as if only then realizing that it had its source in a human she stopped rocking the child, and raised her head up to gaze at his face. She was wearing a sari now instead of a frock, bright peacock blue with a golden hem, and had several plastic bangles on both her arms. Her long black hair, newly washed, was pulled back into a severe bun that drew her tea-colored skin tightly across her face, and accentuated the large black eyes that stared up at him. Dinesh looked back at her for some time before realizing that in order to communicate he would have to speak.

Sister, he said. Where is your father?

Ganga stared at him without any change in her expression. She shrugged, and then resumed rocking the baby, bringing it closer now to her chest. Both its eyes were open but instead of the sounds or movements normal babies made when they were awake it remained completely still, as though unbothered to begin the ordinary child's struggle of coming to terms with life.

Your father wanted to speak with me.

Ganga looked up at him again and this time a flicker crossed her face.

You're Dineshkanthan.

Dinesh nodded, unsure if he was being asked or told. He waited for her to say something more but she simply continued looking at him.

Do you know where your father is?

If you're Dineshkanthan then my father was searching for you the whole afternoon. He couldn't find you anywhere. Didn't you know he was looking for you?

Dinesh shook his head. I didn't know. I spoke to him in the morning. I was working in the clinic the whole afternoon, and just now I went for a quick walk, he must have missed me.

A walk?

Yes. To the seaside.

To the seaside? She blinked several times. What for?

No reason. Dinesh tried to smile. Just to look at the sea.

For a moment Ganga didn't seem to know what to say. Her eyebrows furrowed, unfurrowed, and furrowed again.

You must be mad.

Dinesh glanced around but no one was paying attention.

I was careful sister, don't worry. I didn't go to the actual beach, I only looked at the sea from the edge of the jungle.

Ganga scanned his face intently, as though looking in it for cracks. Her eyebrows furrowed again and her voice became demanding.

You're Dineshkanthan, aren't you?

Dinesh tried to nod convincingly. And your name is Gangeshwari, no?

She ignored the question. What's your village?

Adampan. In Mannar.

Are you in the camp by yourself?

Dinesh nodded.

Your family?

He shook his head to indicate that he was alone.

Where are you staying?

Just northeast of the camp. In the jungle.

You don't sleep in the camp?

No. But close by. Less than twenty minutes from here.

Ganga looked back down at the baby, as though there was nothing else to say. She brought it up to her face and pressed her nose to its cheek. Its eyes stayed open, but it made no reaction. It looked like an inanimate, human-shaped object onto which living eyes had been grafted.

Whose child is that?

She shrugged.

Is it a boy or a girl?

Girl. She motioned to a young gray-haired woman who was sleeping on the ground a few meters away. That woman looks after it, but she's not the mother.

Dinesh stared at the child. Is something wrong with it? It doesn't look well.

Ganga stood up slowly, and shielding the baby from Dinesh took a few steps away. She looked around her, then half turned towards him from a distance.

If my father couldn't find you he must have gone back to the clinic to stay with the Iyer. Wait a minute, I'll come with you.

She walked over to the sleeping woman and prodded her in the side of the stomach till she stirred and sat up. She deposited the child into the woman's arms, then without turning back or waiting began walking in the direction of the clinic. Dinesh watched as she skillfully skirted the people, tents, and things in her path, then realizing he was meant to follow struggled to catch up with her. He had seen Mr. Somasundaram watching over the Iyer in the clinic that morning, shortly after he'd made the proposal, but only now for some reason did Dinesh realize that it was in the hope the priest would be well enough to perform the marriage rites. For two days the priest had been lying shirtless on a tobacco sack on the clinic floor, a small shard of steel embedded in the side of his chest. He could inhale without issue, but was able to exhale only in fits and starts. He would take air in slowly, in order to prolong as far as possible the painless half of the breathing cycle, and then when he was done inhaling he would pause in preparation for breathing out, not having allowed his lungs to fill to even a third of their capacity for fear of having too much air to expel. The pause was followed by a sudden jerk, a premeditated attempt to exhale everything out all at once, and this invariably petered out into a slow, painful struggle to remove the air remaining inside his chest. At the end of each cycle small dark bubbles bloated up in the corners of the Iyer's lips, and depending on the volume of air expelled, either gently receded or burst. All in all it didn't seem the priest would last very long, let alone be capable of performing any marriage rites, but all the same Mr. Somasundaram dutifully wiped away the trickle from the old man's cheek, and swatted away the flies that kept reconvening around his wound. Flies congregated around almost every bit of exposed flesh in the clinic, but it was only when he saw Mr. Somasundaram swatting them away from the priest that morning that Dinesh had noticed how much like temple-goers their ritual was when they set foot on a person's skin. They would fold back their wings so respectfully when they landed, bending their four back legs, lowering their bodies, and bowing down their heads. Raising their two front legs up in front of their faces they would rub their little hands together silently as if in fervent prayer, and only after several seconds of prostrating like this would they put their lips down reverently to the skin.

As Dinesh and Ganga neared the area in front of the clinic, negotiating the slippery earth between the tarpaulins and all the splayed hands and feet, their movement became more tentative. Whenever he could Dinesh looked up from the ground to watch Ganga moving carefully in front of him, her hands daintily holding up the bottom of her sari so its edges didn't drag through the muck. He was glad that they had stopped talking, that for a while at least they could be silent. It wasn't that their conversation had gone poorly or unpleasantly, for in truth he'd been in too much a state of shock to have been aware of what he was saying to Ganga or to have noticed its effect on her face. He had been too astonished by the fact that thoughts were escaping his mouth in the form of sounds and entering her head by way of her ears to have paid attention to anything else while they were talking, and was grateful now simply for the chance to spend some time in silence, recovering. He hadn't taken into consideration the fact that he and Ganga could talk, that they could communicate, and that being married would mean or at least involve speech. He couldn't think of any examples, it was true, but there could be no doubt that marriage involved not only the occasional sharing of information but also conversation, speaking simply for the sake of speaking. The thought troubled Dinesh vaguely, since he didn't really know what they would be able to talk about when the time came, but most likely, he knew, he was troubled only because he'd gotten so used to being silent in the recent past. It was only natural he would find speaking strenuous, even a little strange, after having gone so long without conversation, and there was no point getting anxious when with a little practice he could probably get accustomed to it once more.

They passed the smaller school building, which still had the words "Staff Room" painted in bold black letters over the doorway, to the long rectangular building that housed most of the injured. The building was partitioned by walls into several classrooms, grades one through nine, each labeled neatly above its entrance just like the staff room, all in full use except eight and nine, which had been damaged the previous week by shelling. The desks and chairs in each room had been removed in order to increase floor space, and the wounded were laid out toe-to-toe, torso-by-torso, on sacks and tarps across the cement floor. The only signs that the rooms had until just recently been used for teaching were the blackboards and the posters still hanging up on the walls, alphabets, times tables, and a few children's paintings. Dinesh and Ganga walked slowly along the façade of the building, taking a quick measure of the situation in each room through the iron grilles meant to provide students with light and fresh air, till they reached the grade-five classroom and stopped cautiously on the threshold. Mr. Somasundaram was in the same place as earlier that day, on the far side of the room beside the opposite wall, crouching over the shirtless body of the priest. A shaft of warm afternoon light fell on the two men through the grille and Dinesh and Ganga stood for a moment watching from the doorway as Mr. Somasundaram, with far less vigor now than in the morning, massaged the Iyer tenderly with his fingertips and thumbs, moving wearily from his neck to his shoulders to his arms, staring dumbly all the while at his own hands as if lost in the rhythm of the movement. Even from afar it was easy to tell that the Iyer's chest wasn't moving, that the pool of blood that filled the space between his upper and lower lips was no longer bubbling. He had passed away at some point without any warning, apparently, and oblivious to this development Mr. Somasundaram had continued tending to his lifeless body. Dinesh waited near the doorway as Ganga walked on tiptoe past all the wounded bodies towards her father, who on seeing her stopped what he was doing and sat up in slight surprise. He looked from his daughter to Dinesh, then turned back to the Iyer, to the unmoving chest and the trickle of dark blood that had hardened on his cheek. He gazed in silence at the body for a moment, then squeezed the lifeless hands, tapped the eyelids, and stood up a little shakily. Wordlessly he walked past his daughter and Dinesh to the entrance, where he paused for a moment and then, directing them to follow, began to head east. They followed silently, Ganga close behind and Dinesh trailing at a distance, their legs moving faster and with more assurance the more distance they put between themselves and the clinic, till arriving back at the tent Mr. Somasundaram came to an abrupt stop. For a while he stared down at a shallow pool of water the brief rain had formed on the ground, then he raised his eyes and looked at Dinesh.

The Iyer has passed away, he started, saying this as if it were something they could not have known by themselves. But it doesn't matter. People can't be expected to follow every single custom in such conditions.

Ganga moved closer to her father. What do you mean? Her voice was low but urgent, as though she didn't want Dinesh to hear. How can we get married without the Iyer?

Mr. Somasundaram's eyes stayed on Dinesh. It can't be helped. We have to do what we have to do. God will punish others more severely for the things they've done.

But why should we even perform the ceremony? It won't make a difference to the army, they won't know. We can just pretend to be married if they ask.

Mr. Somasundaram didn't seem to hear the question. She repeated the last part but he made no response, simply stood there staring down at the puddle in front of him, thinking what exactly it was impossible to say. Ganga looked at her father half in earnest and half in disbelief. She studied his face, as though searching it for something she'd been able to take for granted till then but could now no longer find, and then without signal her eyes glazed over. The sharp, shapeless points at their centers disappeared into the liquid of her irises, and though no circles formed under her eyes and no creases deepened on her face she seemed, suddenly, by some subtle change, a little older. She turned abruptly and started walking north. Mr. Somasundaram continued staring at the puddle for a while and then, as though waking from a dream, his features hardened. He indicated to Dinesh that he should remain near the tent and turned to walk after Ganga. That there was some kind of issue between the two of them there could be no doubt, but it was best, Dinesh knew, to avoid jumping to conclusions. He watched as they advanced into the distance, the father catching up gradually with the daughter, till reaching her finally he grabbed her by the arm so that she stopped moving. They were quite far away and with all the tents and people in between it was difficult to make out precisely what was happening, but from what could be seen they didn't appear to be talking. They were simply standing there beside each other it seemed, neither one of them looking at the other.

Dinesh turned away, slightly restless. In front of him was the large, square tent that belonged to Ganga and Mr. Somasundaram, its blue tarpaulin covering sagging slightly between the poles. It covered a larger area than the tents nearby and likely contained a small dugout inside too, so the family could take cover immediately when shells began to rain down. It was where Ganga and Mr. Somasundaram had slept for the last few weeks, where all four members of the family had stayed while the mother and son were still alive, and probably it was where they kept all the possessions they had been able to bring with them from home. Why exactly he couldn't say but Dinesh felt a longing to go inside. By entering the tent and looking closely at whatever it contained he would somehow be better able to understand what was going on, he felt. He glanced up again at Ganga and Mr. Somasundaram.

They were too far away to be able to pay any attention to him, and if
he were careful he might even be able to tell when they were coming
back and get out before they saw him. Even if he wasn't he could always make up an excuse when the time came, for the chance to inspect
everything inside the tent unhindered would not come again, and it felt
too precious to miss. Taking care not to touch the tarpaulin more
than necessary, Dinesh crouched down close to the entrance. He hesitated for a moment, then insinuated his head into the narrow opening.
The air inside was stiff and dry, slightly stale, and the blue light filter-
ing in made everything there seem outside time. There was a bedsheet
spread out neatly over the area near the entrance, beneath it a sheet
of white tarpaulin to keep it from getting wet when there was rain. A
beige bag lay at the bedsheet's center, its canvas fabric bursting on
both sides with the volume of things inside. Along one side of the
tent there was a battered plastic suitcase and a smaller canvas bag,
and along the other side a few blackened pots and pans, some plastic
bags containing rice and other dry food, and another plastic bag holding a few slippers and shoes. At the far end of the tent was the dugout,
more than four feet deep from what he could see, its sides reinforced by
thin wooden beams. Inching further into the tent so that half his body
was inside, Dinesh moved toward the bag on the bedsheet and looked
at it intently, as if it were possible to glean from it some hidden truth.
He wanted to open it up and look inside but it felt slightly risky, since
it required that he enter the tent more completely, and what excuse
would he have if Ganga and Mr. Somasundaram returned suddenly
and found him there like that? He could of course open the bag and
rifle through its contents very quickly, so the whole thing would be over
before they could possibly return, but that was pointless since whatever it was he wanted to discover would surely require more time to

unearth than a mere perusal allowed. Dinesh shuffled in a little further, so that his knees were resting on the sheet, while his feet still remained outside. Reaching forward with both hands, he let his fingertips graze the sides of the swollen bag, and then, slightly more at ease, caress the stretched fabric. He divined the edges of the things outlined lightly against the surface, and pressed into them softly with his palms, in an effort to envisage what they might be. He couldn't tell with any certainty, but no longer worried about being caught he cradled the bag between his hands, and closing his eyes listened, as though the bag were the belly of a woman with child, for the faintest intimations of life, grateful if he could discern even a hint of the things that were inside, as if by means of them he could come to a better understanding of the situation.

Whatever she and her father were in disagreement about, Ganga was right that getting married would make no great difference to her safety. The two of them could always just pretend to be married if it made a difference to how the soldiers treated her, and the chances were good that they would do with her what they wanted in any case, regardless of her marital status. Why Mr. Somasundaram was so anxious for them to get married, then, if this was how things stood, was a little difficult to say. It was possible naturally that he just wanted to see his daughter married before he died, so he could know she wouldn't be left alone if he didn't survive, but this was implausible too since getting married now, he must have known, would more likely hurt Ganga's prospects than help. Most probably they would both be killed before the fighting was finished, but on the off chance that she survived while he died she would be forced to live out the rest of her life a widow, whereas if she stayed unmarried there was a chance at least that she could find a husband by herself later on. Getting married was

not necessarily in Ganga's best interests, therefore, and if Mr. Somasundaram wanted her married it could not have been for her sake but
his own. Probably it was something he wanted only so he could be
free from responsibility for the last member of his family, so that being
no longer responsible for anyone, he'd be able to dwell on his shame
alone at last and in peace. That Mr. Somasundaram felt such shame
there could be no doubt, after all. It was a father's duty to keep his
family members safe, and he had failed to keep safe his wife and son.
No doubt he had done everything he could, which meant that he could
in some sense feel free of guilt, but the fact it had been totally beyond
his power to save them probably only made him feel worse, all things
considered, not better. What right did he have after all to take on the
responsibilities of a husband and father if he could not even guarantee the safety of his wife and son? Whether or not another man might
have fared any better in his position was beside the point, for what right
did he have to get married and have children if he couldn't provide
them with what mattered most? The world had been unfair to him it
was true, it had led him to believe he could take on these duties and
then removed all possibility of doing so, while letting others who'd
taken the same risk go on with their lives untroubled, but regardless
of this, at the end of the day, each person had to answer for what they
had, as individuals, undertaken. Whether or not one had been able to
keep safe one's loved ones was what mattered, nothing else, and he,
in the end, had not. It was only natural if what he wanted above all
now was to be absolved of his last responsibilities, so he could have
the leisure at least to reflect quietly on his failings as a man.

By marrying his daughter off people would say that Mr. Somasundaram was forsaking her of course, passing his duties off onto somebody else simply so he could rest more easily till the end. Perhaps that

was why Ganga was upset, because she felt that her father was abandoning her. It wasn't necessarily the case that she disliked Dinesh, or even that she didn't want to marry him, and perhaps, in a different situation, she would even have agreed to the marriage gladly, without hesitation. It was difficult to say for sure, but however things stood with Ganga it was hard at the same time not to feel a little sympathy for Mr. Somasundaram too. He was renouncing the duties of a father to his daughter it was true, and this was something that couldn't be excused, but didn't the fact that he was taking so much trouble to make arrangements before taking leave of her, instead of just abandoning her all of a sudden one day, mean that he saw himself still as bound to her in some way? Whether or not he stayed by her side there was no denying he could no longer protect her, he depended much more on her in fact than she did on him, and yet he still felt responsible for her future. Even if he was trying to transfer this responsibility he still felt that it was his to transfer, believed that it would remain his until finally transferred, which meant he still saw Ganga as his daughter, in a sense, and even if more might be asked of a father at the end of the day, it still meant something, Dinesh felt, in such a situation, to feel that way. A month or so before he had seen, not in the present camp but in one of the camps where he had been staying before, two men in their late thirties viciously kicking a man on the ground while the latter's wife and young son looked on, whimpering loudly but keeping their distance. The man on the ground could hardly move, he reeled with every kick and was coughing up thick gobs of blood, was almost choking by the time a few men who'd seen what was happening came and physically restrained the attackers. The two men struggled to free themselves so they could let themselves loose on the man again, but held back forcefully their anger gradually subsided, and breathing heavily they explained what had happened to the crowd that had gathered around them. The man they were beating was their brother-in-law, and had been married to their younger sister for a few years by that point. He had always been a somewhat nervous man, had somehow never seemed fully dependable or trustworthy, and when the fighting got bad each of them separately began to worry he might abandon their sister and nephew and run away in order to escape his responsibilities. They never said anything obviously, they had felt ashamed to suspect someone in their family without good reason, but then waking up that same morning they found, all of a sudden, that he had disappeared. They waited several hours but he didn't come back, and finally the two of them set out through the camp to try to find him. When they found him at last he was lying on the ground half-conscious, far away from their tent, a canister of pesticide half-empty beside his body. Even running away was too demanding for the coward and so instead he'd tried to kill himself, leaving them to take care of his wife and child instead of confronting the situation himself, as a real husband and father ought to. Hearing all this the men that were holding the brothers relaxed their grips a little without letting go, and tried to draw them away from the man on the ground. If they killed him they'd be giving him exactly what he wanted, one of them said calmly as he pulled them away, and anyway there was too much death already without civilians starting to kill each other too. When they were gone at last the man's wife, too afraid to show her husband any affection in front of her brothers, knelt down on the ground next to him and began wiping away the blood on his face, crying silently with their son who'd heard everything his uncles had said but was too young, hopefully, to understand what any of it meant.

Footsteps were approaching the tent, and Dinesh's hands froze on the bag's surface. The footsteps paused immediately outside the tent, but then thankfully continued on their way. Dinesh loosened his grip on the bag. He was a little reluctant to leave the tent, since in addition to the bag there were other things he hadn't had a chance to give sufficient attention to, but he'd spent several minutes inside already, and it was best he leave well before Ganga and Mr. Somasundaram returned. He took a last look around, tried to memorize the arrangement of everything inside so its secrets might be revealed to him at a later time, then slowly backed out into the vastness of the evening. The sky was already darkening, but there was something overwhelming about the giant gray expanse that opened out overhead after having been inside the small, square covering of the tent. Dinesh stayed on the ground some time while his eyes adjusted, then stood up in a slight daze and looked around. He scanned the area till he saw Ganga and Mr. Somasundaram walking slowly back towards the tent, the father in front and the daughter a few feet behind. Neither of them seemed to be paying much attention to their surroundings, and they almost certainly hadn't realized he'd been inside. Dinesh turned around and pretended for a while to be staring at something on the ground, and then when their footfall was near enough for him to hear he turned towards them with a look of slight surprise, as though his mind had till then been occupied by something other than themselves.

Son, said Mr. Somasundaram. His voice was calm now, authoritative, different from how he'd sounded earlier. Come. You still want to go ahead with the marriage, no?

Dinesh looked at Ganga, who stood a few feet to the right. She was looking away, and nothing of the expression on her face could be seen. Dinesh turned back to Mr. Somasundaram. He hesitated a moment, then slowly nodded.

Good. There is no longer a priest to do the marriage rites. And there's no way to get a formal registration. But the main thing, said Mr. Somasundaram, is that as father of the bride, I am giving you both my blessing.

He turned from Dinesh to his daughter, who was still looking away.

The circumstances are unusual, but this is a marriage just like any other. You must stay together, look after each other, and be responsible for one another. And one day, like in any ordinary marriage, you must have children and raise a family.

Neither of them said anything in response. Mr. Somasundaram crouched down in front of the tent that Dinesh had just been inside, reached in, and took out the tightly packed beige bag that Dinesh had just been holding. He unzipped the bag and took out from it various things that he laid out on the floor of the tent near its entrance, two cardboard folders stuffed with various documents, plastic bags, folded clothes, and several neatly packed paper parcels, all of them somehow very different from anything Dinesh could have imagined as being inside the bag. From near the bottom finally Mr. Somasundaram got out what he was searching for, a small, framed picture of Lakshmi, and a paper envelope with a small lump inside it. He put the other things back into the bag and tried to zip it shut, though in his hurry he hadn't packed them in compactly enough and was unable to close the opening completely. He placed the bag a few feet in front of the tent, and propped up the picture against it so that it stood almost vertically. He stood up slowly, looked around to make sure nobody was within earshot, then spoke in a hushed voice to Dinesh.

There is nine thousand rupees in the bag and the deeds to our land in Malayaalapuram. There are saris and other valuables too, all my wife's jewelry. Everything belongs to both of you now. Look after it carefully. It isn't much, but nobody can say I didn't give you everything I had.

He began to peel open the envelope he had taken out of the bag. Careful not to rip the paper more than necessary, he took out from inside it a folded children's handkerchief. He put the envelope in his shirt pocket and laid the folded handkerchief out reverently on his left palm. Opening it out slowly with his right hand he revealed to them, threaded on slender yellow twine, no larger than a child's little toe, a small, dense, intricately wrought piece of gold.

This, said Mr. Somasundaram, holding up the necklace by both ends so the little piece of gold dangled before them, is your mother's thaali.

Dinesh and Ganga stared at the object as though neither had seen a thaali before. They looked at it with a slight nervousness, as though unsure of the item's origin and function, as if it might be possessed of magical powers that could suddenly be let loose upon them.

When you're ready, said Mr. Somasundaram looking at Dinesh, all you have to do is tie the thaali around the bride.

Dinesh looked from Ganga to her father. He noticed that two or three other people nearby were watching them with silent, curious faces, having understood somehow that there was going to be a marriage. He became aware for the first time of his soiled clothes, his grimy body.

Shouldn't I wash first? I didn't know we were going to perform the marriage this very moment. I don't have any other clothes to wear.

Don't worry son, said Mr. Somasundaram. It doesn't matter. To tie the thaali you only need the blessings of the bride's parents, the bride's father. In circumstances like this we don't have to worry about anything else.

He held out the thaali to Dinesh, who took it uncertainly in both hands, and he motioned for Ganga to sit down before Lakshmi. She squatted down, careful not to dirty her sari, and sat there gazing list-lessly at the goddess. Dinesh stepped between Ganga and the picture, and standing stiffly with the thaali in both hands, looked nervously at Mr. Somasundaram, who nodded for him to go on. He got slowly to his knees so that his bride's head was level with his chest, averting his eyes but vividly aware at the same time of her nearness. Her hair smelled sharply of soap and oil, her sari of mothballs, the sari too, per-haps, being from her parents' wedding. Taking an end of the twine in each hand, Dinesh let the little piece of gold rest softly on the smooth brown skin between Ganga's collarbones, and carefully brought both ends of the string round her neck. He paused, as though in anticipa-tion of some strange transformation that would occur upon the tying of the two ends, and then, breathing deeply in and leaning gently over Ganga, careful not to touch her skin, he tied the first knot, then the second, and finally the third. He paused, still holding the string, then leaned back and let it fall. For a moment their eyes met; the world outside the line of their gaze seemed to melt away, and as two humans crossing paths in a lifeless and empty land will stop and with words and gestures attempt to build a narrow bridge between their worlds, they locked their eyes together and tried, if only for a brief and trembling second, to break through the dead skin and dusty air that lay between them.

A light breeze brushed past their ears. They were married.

3

WOULD YOU LIKE TO go for a walk?

The question, though voiced softly, rang out in the silence, and both Dinesh and Ganga became aware suddenly of their surroundings. The half circle of the moon was visible already in the sky, and the darkness of evening had gathered round their bodies like a warm ocean, washing over them in slow, gentle waves. How long the two of them had been standing there, just a few feet from each other yet completely still, it was impossible to say. After the thaali had been tied and the small number of onlookers had dispersed they had stood there watching for some time as Mr. Somasundaram scoured the tent, as he repacked the beige bag that he'd given them, and made sure that everything else was in its proper place. When the tent was as neat and empty as a house ready for fresh tenants he had climbed out, taken a few steps back from the scene, and contemplated his son-in-law and daughter together from a distance, the tent behind them, and the beige bag by their feet. Under no circumstance should they let themselves be separated from one another, he had instructed Dinesh. If they came into contact with recruiters from the movement or government soldiers they should display Ganga's thaali at once, so there would be no doubt that they were husband and wife. They should say they'd been married for a year, and if they were asked to produce the marriage certificate they should say it had been lost while evacuating the village. Dinesh had nodded, slightly confused about why these possibilities needed to be discussed so soon, and as though in explanation Mr. Somasundaram added that he had to head back to the clinic, that he had to be there to ensure the Iyer's body was being dealt with appropriately. His body slackened a bit as he said this, and the tense expression on his face loosened. He looked at the two of them as if in admiration of the last touches on a picture he'd just completed, then leaned forward and tried to kiss Ganga, who stayed stiff as he put his hands around her head and pressed his cheeks to her face. Picking up the smaller canvas bag that Dinesh had seen inside the tent earlier he looked the two of them over once more, then turned with a kind of finality and began to walk away, not towards the clinic but in a southwesterly direction instead. The two of them had continued standing there, eyes averted, neither of them certain what to say or do, till finally Dinesh had begun to worry that too much time had passed without speech or movement. The momentum created by the tying of the thaali had to be absorbed into some other joint activity, he felt, otherwise their marriage would come to a standstill, and stretching his arms to signal that he was getting a little restless, he had readied himself, then finally spoken.

Ganga raised her head at last in response.

Walk? Where to?

Dinesh tried to make eye contact. I can show you the place I stay.

Ganga thought for a moment.

We have to watch the bag until my father comes back.

Why don't we just take it with us?

Don't be silly. What about the tent? We can't leave it unwatched.

It'll be okay, Dinesh tried to say with confidence. We'll be back soon, before anyone knows.

Ganga was silent a while longer, as though weighing the suggestion against other plans she'd envisioned for the evening, and then assented. Dinesh picked up the bag and led the way slowly northeast through the camp. He listened with wonder to the delicate footsteps behind him but also with slight apprehension, as if only a very slender thread held the two of them together and there was a chance, if he walked too fast, that the thread might snap. He maintained a deliberately slow pace, therefore, even as they reached the outskirts of the camp, happy in any case to postpone the moment they would have to stand once more in front of each other with nothing to say. They passed the northeastern boundary of the camp, and made their way through the jungle for a short distance, negotiating the low branches and pulling aside the leathery vines till unexpectedly, in a section where the canopy was especially dense, a small circular clearing opened out in front of them. It was getting late already but there was enough space between the surrounding trees for the evening's last blue light to illuminate the ferns and shrubs that blanketed the ground, and stopping at its cusp, Dinesh stepped aside so Ganga could survey the place in its entirety. On the far side, partially obscured by the vegetation around it, was the long elliptical rock beside which he slept each night, four or five feet long and about two feet tall near the center, its entire surface soft and mossy like a sheet of dry green carpet. Realizing as soon as he saw it that the space would be ideal for sleeping he had cleared away all the plants immediately in front of the rock, creating a narrow rectangular space shaded by the tall fronds of the surrounding ferns, indiscernible even from the edges of the clearing. Painstakingly he had plucked away each blade of grass in the rectangle, then all the pebbles and stones embedded in the soil, using the latter to create a decorative border around the area, a kind of psychological or spiritual fortification for his sleeping space. He used a few sticks to mark the bed out even more concretely but feeling then that it had become too conspicuous, that someone who saw it would be able to tell that the space was inhabited, he removed the sticks so that only the border of pebbles and stones remained. Last of all he sculpted a gentle mound of earth in front of the north-facing end of the rock, so that his head had a pillow to lie on while the rest of his body was bedded by the rich, soft soil he'd taken so much trouble to uncover. His back pressed against the rock, not for the softness its mossy surface provided but for the sense of security it gave him, the reassurance that no danger could approach from the side to which his back was turned, he would lie down each night in this rectangle silently and without sleeping, neither thinking nor waiting, and looking at it now, at the mossy rock and the vegetation between which it was cushioned, and the tall trees within which these themselves were nestled, Dinesh felt a strange flush of warmth spread across his cheeks, neck, and arms. He had felt safe and comfortable in the clearing before, but looking at it now with Ganga beside him it seemed to him there could be no safer or more comforting place anywhere else in the camp.

Ganga regarded the area for a while and then looked back at Dinesh as though unsure what he wanted her to do. Dinesh beckoned her to follow him and walked towards the rock, taking care not to step on any of the plants on the way. He crouched down in front of it, put the bag down to his right so that Ganga could sit down without getting her sari dirty, and motioned for her to join him. She came to where he sat without a word, and seeing that he wanted her to sit on the bag, picked up the hem of her sari and crouched down on it lightly. She said nothing, unsurprised or uninterested apparently to find the lovingly cultivated sleeping space hidden there, as though there was in the little rectangle nothing special, no quality worthy of remark. Perhaps she simply needed to spend more time there. Perhaps the worth of the place was something that took time to appreciate, something that wasn't obvious immediately. It was strange after all how attached he himself had come to be to it. The war had scattered and killed his family, relatives, and friends, and he had ended up in this particular camp, found within it this particular place, when it could just as easily have been some other place in some other location. He had spent no more than eight, maybe nine nights here, and still for some reason he'd come to feel so close to it, especially to this bed where each night he lay, silent and still, unsleeping. It was as if in the hours he'd spent there his body had shed some warm, imperceptible substance into the earth and stone, something that filled the little space with an understanding of him, so it had become in a way a part of him, a special place, a home almost. What exactly he might have shed it was hard to say—a scent perhaps, perhaps old skin. Perhaps it was just the murmuring of his body from previous nights, just the faint traces of his bodily rhythms vibrating still through the particles of earth and stone. Perhaps it was just these echoes of the body, resounding in the places a person has been long after they have gone, that made a place a person's home, and perhaps the slight shiver one has in returning to a childhood home was due only to them, due simply to the sudden resonance of the body's living pulsations with the pulsations that had been imparted to the place long before, as when a tuning fork strikes a full-bodied object, is taken away, and then before its trembling fades is brought beside it again. What exactly it was that drew him close to the rock and the bed it was difficult to say, but he could sense or smell or feel that the place cared for him, that it would take care of him. Ganga would come to feel this way also perhaps, and if she didn't at present it was all right, it was okay, for the place, he felt sure, would take her in and keep her safe anyway.

A wave of cool air passed over the clearing and the ferns around them stirred slightly then stilled. Dinesh became aware once more of the fact that Ganga was physically beside him. He hadn't yet had the chance to look at her properly he realized, to study her face so he could know what kind of person she was and how she was feeling. When they were talking earlier he had been too distracted, and then when they were standing together in silence after having been married he had been too shy to look at her directly. He shifted his body towards her a little now and tried, without being obvious, to study her through the corner of his eye. She was leaning forward on the bag and her face was angled away from him, staring into the distance. From his position on the ground below he couldn't make out her expression, all he could see was the gentle arch of her long back and the way the edge of her blouse's blue sleeve coiled tightly around her left arm. He leaned back against the rock with an exaggerated movement, hoping to catch her attention somehow.

That's a beautiful sari, he said loudly.

Ganga nodded her head, her face still pointed away.

Is that your mother's too?

She nodded once more, and picked up one of the little stones from the border of the bed in front her, began rolling it lightly across the palm of her left hand. Running along her forearm, Dinesh noticed, was a long, elevated scar, lighter than the rest of her skin and smooth apart from a few slightly distended serrations perpendicular to its length. He sat up and instinctively brought his right hand next to it, his fingertips hovering close to her skin without quite touching it.

Ganga stopped playing with the stone.

When did you get that? Dinesh asked.

She didn't answer at once, as though she couldn't tell immediately. It happened some time ago. I jumped into a bunker without looking.

Does it hurt still?

Can't you see it's healed?

I have a wound like that too, but sometimes it still hurts. Dinesh stretched out his left leg and lifted up his sarong to show a laceration that extended from the back of his knee down to just above the heel. Unlike hers it did not protrude out from the skin but was sunken in and of a shiny, almost polythene consistency. It's from a piece of shrapnel.

Ganga looked at his scar, looked at her own, then turned back to the stone she'd been rolling on her palm. It was hard for Dinesh to know whether she could understand any of the things he said, or whether for that matter she even understood her own words. She had a habit of squinting slightly and pausing before she said anything, her eyes far away, searching, and when at last she spoke her words seemed detached, as if coming from a source external to her, from muscles moving mechanically in her tongue, mouth, and throat. Furrowing her brows she would listen to these words as intently as he did, as though she herself was somehow clueless about what she had just said.

Perhaps he was the same way too, when he spoke, it was hard to say. Dinesh lowered his sarong and crossed his legs. He shifted back towards the rock, leaned against the dry, mossy surface as if to get some rest, and then glancing once more at Ganga, felt again the urge to speak. If he waited too long it would be difficult to resume talking he was afraid, each of them would fall back into their separate worlds, and the conversation would come to a permanent end.

How far are you in your studies?

Ganga opened her lips as if about to say something and then closed them again. She let the stone lie still in her hand and then put it down, almost reluctantly, on the ground between them. It was unclear from her face whether she hadn't heard the question properly, whether she'd heard the question but hadn't understood, or whether she'd understood its meaning but simply didn't know what to say. She stared at the ground for a while before her lips moved finally and a few words, scarcely audible, came out.

I finished O-levels a year ago.

Did you start studying for A-levels?

She nodded slowly. But school closed a few weeks after starting.

In Malayaalapuram, no?

She nodded.

What school did you go to?

Malayaalapuram Hindu Girls' College.

Dinesh paused for a moment on hearing this, then searched for another question.

What path were you on?

Accounts.

Were you good at maths?

Ganga thought for a moment and then her eyebrows furrowed in irritation.

How should I know?

Dinesh was still for a while, then picked up the stone that Ganga had put down and examined it in his hand. He held it between his thumb and forefinger and pressed hard, felt its rough, uneven edges against his fingertips, surprised almost that it didn't melt or crumble under the pressure he exerted.

I did science, he said quietly.

Ganga didn't respond.

I came second in my A-level batch. The only boy ahead of me in the district got a place at university. I missed by only a few marks.

He waited for her to say something but she didn't look up.

My favorite subject was biology.

Again there was no response. Dinesh put the pebble back in its place on the border of the bed. He felt slightly foolish, as though he had just betrayed some kind of ignorance or stupidity. Why he'd asked about her studies of all things he didn't know. He hadn't thought of school life in so long, and then suddenly those words had come out of him, A-levels, university, maths, biology. They'd come out almost involuntarily, and as soon as he heard them he'd felt the great distance between him and them, as with a photo from childhood in which one's face is recognizable, while the mood and thoughts that must have animated it have gone. School and exams had been part of his life of course, had been part of how he'd lived, but what reason was there to talk about his past now, or to ask Ganga to tell about hers? They had left them behind so long ago, what was the point in speaking of them, what relevance did their pasts have to who they were now? Dinesh thought of all the abandoned and destroyed buildings he used to play in as a child, many years before, not long after the movement had liberated his village and the surrounding area for the first time, when he would climb in quietly over the half-collapsed palm leaf fences, through the wild, disused gardens, and wander into the interiors of all the broken structures. The crumbling walls would be sprayed with bullet holes, and where they weren't completely perforated the orange brick would be visible like bleeding wounds. Moving about silently he would wade through all the dust and debris, poking and prodding the broken terracotta tiles from caved-in roofs, the rotting wooden planks from doors and ceilings, the shattered ceramic basins, the warped, rusting iron of foundations and reinforcements. There were dozens of damaged buildings near his home to explore, but no matter how different their character or purpose had been, whether they were once houses, shops, schools, or shrines, the rubble of all the buildings ruined by the fighting had always looked the same. You could find, of course, among the fragments of plaster, concrete, wood, and brick, things that taught you about what the buildings had been, about who they had housed and what purpose they had served. The remains of a desk at which a child had once sat and studied, the rusted shell of a pot or kettle in a lost family's kitchen, or the tarnished brass bell and broken plaster sculpture of a roadside temple. But apart from these small, useless vestiges of their histories, the war had reduced all these buildings to the same state, and so what use was there really in combing through the ruins? What point could there be, except for childish curiosity, in trying to learn the identity of these destroyed structures, what point was there when the best thing would have been to clear away all the rubble, to raze whatever was left, and build in its place whatever was necessary for the future, completely new?

But if they couldn't talk about their pasts, what could they say to each other at all, given that there was no future for them to speak of either?

The leaves rustled softly around them, and Dinesh looked again at Ganga. She was looking down still and it was impossible to tell if she was still annoyed. He spoke in a quiet voice.

Are you happy we're married?

She looked at him and mumbled something he couldn't understand.

If you like, he went on, we can have a proper wedding later on.

Ganga remained silent for a while, then suddenly stood up.

Are you hungry?

Dinesh looked up at her slightly surprised. He had hardly eaten in the last few days but had grown used to being hungry, and hadn't even thought about finding something to eat. He stood up and fumbled with his sarong, which had become loose from being seated.

I have to cook some rice for my father, said Ganga. I'll make some for you too.

Dinesh smiled awkwardly, embarrassed by the offer.

It isn't necessary.

It won't make any difference.

Dinesh thought a moment, and then moved his head in acquiescence. He picked up the beige bag and walked to the edge of the clearing. He turned round to make sure Ganga was following, waited till she was behind him, then entered the darkness of the quietly stirring canopy. Why exactly she had suggested making food for him he wasn't sure. Most likely it was because she had to cook for her father as she had said, but he was worried it might also be because she felt sorry for him. Perhaps she'd inferred from the fact that he had no belongings that he had no money for food, or perhaps she could tell by how thin he was that he hadn't been eating. Maybe he should refuse the food she offered him, say that he'd eaten earlier in the day and wasn't really hungry, though thinking about the prospect of food now he wasn't sure he would be able. The last proper meal he'd had had been two days earlier, a few handfuls of watery rice from an old woman he'd helped dig a bunker for a month or two before. She had recognized him as he was walking through the camp and had called out to him loudly, almost cheerfully. It took a moment for Dinesh to recollect who she was, for she had been reunited with the rest of her family since he'd last seen her, and her face was much brighter and fuller, less rigidly clenched than in his memory of her. He'd gotten much thinner than when she'd seen him last the woman said, pulling him down by the elbow to make him sit, he should eat with them, the energy would be more useful in his body than in hers. She took some rice from their pot, which was meant not only for her but also her daughter, son-in-law, and grandchild, and served it to him on a folded piece of newspaper. A kilo of rice was already almost a thousand rupees because of the shortage of food, and most evacuees were eating less than a single meal a day. Embarrassed by the woman's generosity and also by the feeling that her son-in-law and daughter would rather not have shared their limited food supply with a stranger, he'd eaten quickly, letting the rice slip down his throat without giving himself the chance to taste or feel it in his mouth, then thanked them and left. The rest of the week he had rationed biscuits from a few packets he'd bought with some of his last money. He ate two in the morning, four in the late afternoon, and another four at night, breaking each biscuit into two or three smaller pieces then soaking them in a little water to soften them and increase their flavor. He took his time grinding each piece into a soft cream in his mouth before letting it go down, though since he ate in only small quantities he hadn't been able to appreciate their taste quite fully.

They emerged from under the trees into the last light of late evening and continued southwest through the camp. There was far less movement now than earlier in the day. Those who could afford it were cooking or eating the food they'd bought from the little that was circulating, and everyone else was sitting silently or trying to sleep in the few hours available to them before the start of the night's shelling. Watching them as they walked by, some faces dimly lit by small, unobtrusive fires, the rest shrouded in the dark-blue shadow of the sky, Dinesh noticed again that hardly anyone in the camp did any talking. A few men and women were whispering to themselves, rocking gently back and forth, quietly laughing, crying, or cursing, but from the vast majority there was only silence. People in the camp communicated of course, they bartered for food and medicine, shared news about the fighting, information about missing people, but these were only practicalities, and when they were communicated everyone more or less ceased speaking. At such times, when there was nothing urgent to be done, no relatives to find or bodies to collect, when the effects of the last bout of shelling had finally been absorbed and there was nothing left to do but wait for the next one, most just sat and marked time in silence. Perhaps they didn't feel like talking. Perhaps they were too tired or too distracted, and simply didn't want to talk any more than needed. It was different in any case from how things were in ordinary life, when people it seemed were always talking to each other in their free time. Relatives would be visiting to chat and gossip, schoolchildren would be laughing and arguing between classes and during intervals. Customers would be staying on in shops and stalls to speak with storekeepers, people stopping on the street to say hello to acquaintances. That in ordinary life people kept talking long past any ostensible need or purpose there could be no doubt, though what they actually spent so much time speaking about Dinesh didn't have any idea. It was as though in all his memories of people talking the mouths were moving but no sounds were coming out. What they might have been saying he couldn't guess, for what after all could there have been to talk about? When the practical concerns of life had been dealt with, when all one's plans had been settled, what was left, really, for anybody to say?

It was possible of course that people kept talking simply because they had to, simply for the sake of talking. Perhaps when people had conversations the subject mattered much less in fact than the act of communicating, and when they didn't have anything urgent or pressing to say they simply looked for other things to talk about, just so they could keep talking. It was difficult to say, but perhaps the real reason that people in ordinary life had subjects to which they always returned in conversation, things that they were interested in and liked learning about, was simply so they had enough material to allow them to keep talking. For even if the act of talking was more important than what was talked about, you could never have a conversation after all unless you had a subject to speak about. And perhaps this was why everyone in the camp remained silent, not because they didn't want to talk, but because they no longer had anything to say. Conversation was a fragile thing after all, like a plant that grows only in rich, warm, nourishing soil. Just as the cells of the human body couldn't survive above and below certain temperatures, just as human eyes couldn't see above and below certain wavelengths of radiation, and human ears couldn't hear above and below certain thresholds of frequency, perhaps there existed also only a narrow range of conditions under which human conversation could flourish. It wasn't that people in the camp didn't want to talk, for human beings would always talk, if they had the opportunity. Conversation was like an unspooling of invisible fiber that was shot into the air as a stream of sound, that entered the bodies of other people through their ears, that went from those humans to others, and from them to yet more. Thoughts, feelings, and conjectures, stories, jokes, and slander were nothing but thinly spun threads that tied the insides of people together long after speaking had ended, so that communities were nothing more than humans held together in this way, in large, intricate, imperceptible webs whose function was not so much to restrict movement as to connect each individual to every other. Needing such a connection people would always find a way to talk, if they could. It was not for this reason that those in the camp had ceased speaking but because, rather, there was simply no longer anything for them to say. The diaphanous threads which in ordinary life had been so easily spun had been dissolved now, leaving nothing left to unspool, and each and every person in the camp had to sit silently alone, lost inside themselves, unable, in any way, to connect.

Ganga motioned to Dinesh to wait outside the tent and then went in alone with the bag. She came out a few minutes later carrying a bundle of dry twigs and sticks in one arm, and an indented metal pot with a fire-blackened base in the other. Instead of her sari she was wearing the loose cotton frock that Dinesh had seen her wearing around the clinic on other days, a faded pink dress stained yellowish brown around the waist and lap. She deposited the wood in a small ashen pit that had been dug just next to the tent, and put the pot down on the ground next to it. She went back into the tent and brought out a plastic bottle and two fully laden plastic bags, one about four times the size of the other. From the larger bag she poured into the pot a significant amount of rice and from the smaller bag, carefully, a handful of dhal, then she walked with the bottle in the direction of the pump well nearby. The queues for water were quite long during the day but dissipated usually by late evening, since most people filled up all their bottles early to avoid having to leave their tents and bunkers at night. Ganga returned with the bottle full in a few minutes and poured the water into the pot, measuring with her index and middle fingers to make sure the water was the right level above the rice. From the tent she brought out a few sheets of old newspaper and a matchbox, and squatting down next to the pit she tore the paper into strips and squares that she crumpled and stuffed into the gaps between the wood. She struck a matchstick, held it patiently to each bit of newspaper, and somehow set them all alight before the matchstick had burned down to her fingertips. The paper curled as it caught flame and soon the wood began to crackle. The smaller pieces sent out tiny sparks and a few started to smolder. Ganga shuffled back a little and watched as the fire grew, her body still and her eyebrows narrowly furrowed into the base of her forehead, one hand smoothing over her hair and the other clasped tightly to her knee. There was no sign of Mr. Somasundaram Dinesh realized, though it had been two hours at least since they'd seen him last. Surely the Iyer's burial hadn't taken so long, if he'd actually gone to the clinic to oversee it at all. He looked at Ganga and hesitated, unsure whether the subject should be brought up or avoided. Leaning forward, he spoke eventually in a soft voice.

Do you know where your father is? Should we go and look for him?

Ganga looked up at him. It isn't necessary, she said at once. We should stay here. He must still be burying the Iyer, it will be difficult to find him.

Are you still going to make food for him?

Ganga nodded. He'll eat it when he comes back.

But shouldn't we go back to the clearing after we eat?

She shook her head dismissively. We need to look after the tent and all the things until he comes back. Plus, my father will get worried if he comes back and can't find us.

She stood up, and picking up two thicker pieces of wood that she'd set aside till then, she laid them in parallel across the top of the pit. Lifting up the pot she balanced it on the two pieces of wood so that the growing fire beneath would lick the base directly.

How long do you think the burial will take? It's already been more than two hours.

Dinesh waited, but Ganga simply continued watching the fire. The smaller sticks were burning up now, glowing briefly and blackening, the tips of the larger ones beginning to catch flame. Embers blew up out of the pit before dying like fireflies a short distance away.

It's just that I'm worried the recruiters will notice us if we stay in the camp for too long. That's why I sleep in the jungle, if I stayed here sooner or later some envious mother would tell them about me, or they'd find me on their own and take me away.

Ganga regarded Dinesh for a moment, as though he were presenting to her a completely new consideration, then turned her gaze back to the flames. The bubbling of water inside the pot was slowly becoming discernible behind the intermittent sputtering of the fire, softly at first and then more substantially. They listened for a while as the sound became deeper and heavier, a reminder of something that was distant now but that nevertheless felt nourishing and safe. Ganga rose to make sure the water was boiling, covered the pot with its lid, then crouched back down and continued watching the fire. Her expression was somewhat uneasy, even troubled. It was as though the stiffness or tautness in her features that had prevented her till then from expressing any feelings had been loosened, rendering her, for a moment, naked. Realizing that he was watching her she looked down so that her face was hidden.

It isn't a big issue, said Dinesh. We can stay here until your father comes back. I can stay hidden for a while in the tent.

No, she said without looking up. You're right, it's best we go back to the clearing. I'll leave my father's food in the tent so he can eat later. I can speak to him in the morning.

They sat in silence for ten or fifteen minutes, listening to the bubbling of the pot, and then at last Ganga wordlessly stood up. Holding the lips of the pot carefully she took it quickly off the fire, and using the lid to control the flow poured out the small excess of frothy water onto the ground. She put the pot back on the fire, went inside the tent, and came out with three plates, a ladle, and a plastic bag. From the bag she sprinkled some white powder into the pot, salt probably, then using the ladle began to stir it into the rice and dhal with strange vigor. Dinesh felt somewhat bad, but he didn't know what he could say. It had been difficult to resist speaking when finally he had found something that felt natural and unforced to say, but in retrospect it would obviously have been better had he not brought her father up at all. Whether or not Ganga realized that he was probably not coming back he didn't know, but in any case it was something she would come to see in her own time, and there was no need to force it upon her needlessly. Long ago when he was a child, he remembered, lying in a field somewhere, staring up at the sky, he had rolled onto his stomach to find that the ground he'd been lying on contained little patches of touch-me-not hidden among the grass. A few of the delicate green leaflets that his body had somehow left untouched were still open, each one scarcely a millimeter broad, but most of the leaflets had curled up tightly around their stalks to protect themselves from his body, leaving only their coarse brown undersides exposed. Immediately he had gotten to his knees and leaning down over them, at an angle so as not to block the sun's caressing light, tried to see whether there was any way to convince them to open up again. Touch-me-nots responded to anything but the tenderest contact by withdrawing as if greatly pained, he knew, but how long it took for the little leaves to open up again he had no idea. He could have pried them open by force if he wanted, but to dismantle the little plant's only way of keeping itself safe, even for its own sake, would have left it feeling more violated than before. The only thing he could do was be patient, to wait until the touch-me-nots unfurled again of their own accord. How long it would take he didn't know, minutes, or hours, or days, but when they did bare themselves up to the atmosphere he would be more careful he had promised himself, would take care to be as soft and gentle with them as the vapor of an exhaled breath.

When the rice and dhal was ready Ganga lifted the pot off the fire and put a small amount of the mixture on a plate for her father, hardly enough for a meal if he were to actually return and eat it. She put the plate in the tent just behind the flaps of the entrance, like a priest leaving an offering of food at the foot of a deity, then carefully closing the flaps handed the water bottle to Dinesh so he could wash his hands. Dinesh poured the water over each hand separately and rubbed his fingers clean while she served a plate for him, then sat down cross-legged where she put his food. He looked up at her to ask her to join him but she shook her head and continued standing there, motioning to indicate that she would eat once he'd started. Dinesh looked down at the steaming food. It had been a long time since he'd eaten from a plate, and he felt somewhat nervous about eating while Ganga looked on. He studied his clean right hand, as though noticing his four fingers and thumb for the first time, then bringing them together he dug into the still-scalding mixture of rice and dhal and began stirring it to allow the heat to dissipate. It was strange feeling his fingers in rice after so long, with the soft wet grains between his fingers right up to the webbing of his hands. It was strange to think that his right hand was used also for eating, that with his hand he was about to put something into his mouth. The rice and dhal fully mixed he gathered up a mouthful delicately in his fingers, hesitated a moment, then brought it to his lips. He opened his mouth, and nudged it in. The food was hot in his mouth, and as he rolled it around with his tongue he savored the shape and taste of the soft grains, his tongue cleaving the rice into separate sections in his mouth then goading it back into a single mass. His jaws moved of their own accord and his molars mushed the rice together, turning the separate grains into a single soft warm whole that slowly made its way to the back of his mouth and was then swallowed, something he became aware of only by the sensation of a warm substance slipping down his throat, past his bulging Adam's apple, down into his gullet. He sat still for a moment, as if in surprise, then gathered the few grains of rice that had been deposited in the recesses of his cheeks and swallowed them too. Letting his tongue move over the sensitive surfaces of his teeth and gums, which he was feeling now as if for the first time, he looked down at his fingers, which were dotted with grains of rice, and took them again to the food on the plate. He gathered more in his hand, brought it to his mouth, chewed it, let it mix, and swallowed once more. His stomach began to burn after a few mouthfuls, probably because it had been so long since he'd eaten this much food at once, but he kept bringing handfuls to his mouth, chewing, mixing, slowly and carefully swallowing, knowing that if he continued eating the pain would soon die down. He began to remember again the rhythm of eating, to recover the proper timing of each part of the sequence, to chew what was in his mouth just as long as it took him to gather together a new handful of rice, and to swallow it in the time it took to bring the newly full hand again to his lips. The rice and dhal on the plate steadily diminished but before it was gone Ganga took the plate from Dinesh, filled it up with more rice and dhal from the pot, and placed it again on the ground before him. She put some of the mixture on another plate then sat down a few feet from him, and hunched over their plates the two of them ate together now, slowly and patiently, each of them fully immersed in the rhythm of eating.

The sky had darkened fully and there was no trace left of the day. Soon the bombing would begin for the night, in an hour or in several, it was impossible to say. They cleaned the last bit of food from their plates, so that nothing could be seen except the wet stainless steel, and for a long time after they finished eating neither of them stirred. From not far away, to the west of where they were seated, rising out of the night, there came a loud, sustained wailing. It sounded at first like a wounded person had woken from the unknowingness of sleep and was being forced to confront their pain consciously again, but as they listened longer to the vigor of the aggrieved voice it seemed to belong not to a wounded person, but rather to someone healthy who'd just been bereaved. And hearing this sound they heard also, as when noticing a single bright star in a sky that previously seemed dull, one becomes aware of the faint glimmer of smaller stars that were till then invisible, they heard also, rising into the night from different points around the camp, other voices, crying, wailing, and moaning, how many exactly it was impossible to say. They rose and fell like ambulance sirens in the distance, some voices dying out as their owners dropped back into unconsciousness and others joining the chorus as their owners came to. Ganga stood up slowly, took their empty plates and the pot, and walked towards the pump well. Standing up, Dinesh licked the last grains of rice off his fingertips and washed his hands once more with water from the bottle, aware that it was time now for them to spend their first night together.

4

WHEN THE FIGHTING ARRIVED Dinesh and his mother too, like everyone else, had packed up their belongings to take with them as they left home. People had been streaming in through the area almost continuously for two or three days, and by the time the movement's order to evacuate sounded out over the village PA system the muted sounds of shelling could already be heard in the distance, exploding heavily and then expanding amply outwards. They spent their last evening looking for a tractor to hire for the journey with two neighboring families, then stayed up the entire night feverishly packing. What exactly they had decided to take with them Dinesh could no longer say, but he could remember still the satisfaction of looking at their mostly empty house when they were finally done, the pleasing thought that no matter what happened their things at least would be safe with them as they headed deeper into the territory. It was not yet light and they had hardly had a moment to reflect on what was happening, but they heaved themselves into the back of the tractor, and perched precariously among all the loosely stacked furniture and possessions, the thin iron walls of the wagon convulsing as the engine sputtered into action, watched almost with curiosity as their calm, quiet lane receded away, as though they were leaving for an unplanned though not necessarily unpleasant holiday. They were too exhausted from the night's work and too sleep deprived to worry strenuously about the situation, and in any case they'd been forced to leave home at various times in the past, being displaced was nothing particularly new. They would be back in only a few weeks probably, no more than a month at the very most. There was a chance the village would see a little gunfire while they were gone, perhaps it would be struck by a few shells too, but most likely they would find their house completely untouched when they returned home.

It was only when they had reached the main road and joined, after a while, the long, disjointed train of evacuees, some of whom had been on the move already for several days, some of whom like them had just left their homes, that it became obvious that this particular evacuation was a little more comprehensive than the ones they'd experienced before. Not just their village but all the territory in the southern parts of their district had been evacuated apparently, and apparently villages all the way in the southeastern corner of the movement's territory too. It was a little surprising, of course, but nobody remarked at length on the matter, for probably it was not worth getting too worried about, probably the movement had just decided to take a few more precautions than usual this time. They moved northeast with the caravan the whole day, till they came to a stop finally at an encampment full of evacuees. How many people were there they couldn't say exactly, but it was larger than any encampment they'd been in on previous evacuations. They stayed there about three weeks, till the shelling drew close again, and they were told then by the movement to pack up their things and move to another encampment, a little further inside the territory. They stayed in the new place another three weeks, moved from that one to another, and from that to yet others, the length of their stays shortening from three weeks to two to ten days to even fewer, till gradually they began to spend more time on the road than in any fixed place. Their pace was slowed by the thousands of new evacuees joining the caravan from every town and village they passed, and the bombing behind them was getting louder with every displacement, but neither this nor any of the other patterns that seemed to be emerging were discussed much or even complained about, for obviously they didn't know all that the movement knew about the situation, and there was no point coming to upsetting conclusions simply for lack of information. Using their tent covers as protection from the sun Dinesh and his mother simply sat in the wagon in uneasy silence as the tractor inched along the crowded copper roads, first northeast and then mainly east, through desert, and scrubland, under endless, almost white-hot sky. Sometimes the road carved its way through sections of jungle, where the dark greens and browns soothed their eyes, where the long, leafy branches of trees on either side of the road entwined above them, creating canopies that let in only cool, speckled light, but sooner or later they would always emerge from these shelters into the vast tracts of hot, dry land, where for hours at a stretch there was nothing to mark their progress except occasional checkpoints, increasingly unmanned, and palmyra trees that still stood erect in the distance.

The other evacuees too brought with them all their belongings, in lorries, tractors, and bullock carts that they had filled to the brim. Plastic and wooden furniture, TVs and sewing machines, cycles and motorbikes, potted plants, mats, broomsticks, pets, poultry, children's toys, anything they could find space for. No matter how close the bombing got most people were unwilling to countenance the possibility of parting with these things, not even when the whistling of the swiftly falling shells behind them became discernible before the explosions, not even when they began to fall indiscriminately on swathes of the packed road. Nobody had expected to be on the move for so many months it was true, nobody could remember the movement having lost this much territory before, but surely it would be only a matter of days before the army would be beaten back, before they would be allowed to return finally to their homes with all the things they had brought. They held on meticulously to each and every possession therefore, using kerosene for fuel when diesel got scarce, navigating past charred bodies and vehicles, persevering until at last the sky darkened, and, heavily and relentlessly, the rain began to fall. Everything that was being transported on tractors and open carts got soaked, even the electronic items that they tried to cover with tarpaulin sheets. The clay roads grew soft and muddy, and the pits deepened and filled to form deep wells of brown water that couldn't be distinguished from puddles. Soon every route was blocked by tractors and lorries that had either been destroyed in the shelling or gotten stuck in the mire. In order to keep moving people were forced to relinquish their vehicles, and with them also all the belongings they had brought so far and at such cost. In states of varying disbelief they cooked their chickens and threw away the cages, piled whatever they could onto the backs of motorbikes or three-wheelers, and continued moving as fast as they could. When for lack of fuel these too had to be abandoned they took only what they could fit inside bags that could be slung around their shoulders or carried by hand, money and jewelry, deeds,

IDs, and photographs, medicine, food, and cooking things, nobody knowing what exactly was most important, and what they would regret leaving behind. Instead of throwing away nice clothes for lack of space some people simply put them on, so that moving wearily among the endless throngs of people, passing blindly all the bodies and belongings abandoned along the muddy roads, from time to time women could be seen wearing bright, colorful saris, green, gold, and magenta, as if returning from a wedding or celebration that had not gone according to plan.

Those who held on to their last bags and bundles till they arrived in the camp could be seen clutching them now at all times. They kept them by their sides when they were awake and asleep, not letting go even when they needed to shit or piss. Not much was in danger of being stolen it was true, since few of the things anyone brought retained any value in the circumstances, but they held to them tightly nevertheless, as if otherwise they would float up and waft away, as if their possessions, whatever purpose they might have served before, had assumed now the role of paperweights. Everybody, of course, at the beginning of their journeys, had been forced to leave things behind. Some people, if their departures had been too sudden or if they hadn't been able to find or afford transport, had been forced to leave behind almost everything. Probably it had been difficult to leave possessions at home, to constantly be wondering whether their things had been looted, but surely they'd taken care to bury or hide the most valuable items in the nooks and crannies of their properties, and in retrospect at least it must have been pleasing to dwell on how safe these things probably still were. So many months and kilometers removed from their homes and villages it must have been satisfying now to think that even if all they'd brought with them had been lost or destroyed, they would still have possessions somewhere in the world, concrete objects that would mark their homes as their own no matter how long they were gone, or who took over in the interim, which would stay constant even as shells came down on their owners and their feelings and memories faded away.

Where exactly his mother and he had been when they were forced to give up their tractor it was hard now for Dinesh to say, but it had probably been in late October or November, shortly before the battle for the movement's capital had begun. They'd been running out of money for some time, but had managed to hold on to the tractor till they reached the home of a distant relative, hoping they'd be able to leave their things inside rather than abandon them by the roadside like other people were doing. They found the house boarded up and locked, it had been evacuated probably just a few days before, and were left with no choice but to unload everything onto the patch of grass in front of the house. They stuffed whatever they would need most urgently into two bags, knowing that most likely they wouldn't again see the things they left behind, then continued their journey on foot, moving, stopping for rest, and when the shells caught up with them moving again. They went on like this for a few weeks, maybe even a month, their movement slow since his mother didn't have the strength to walk for long periods at a stretch, hesitant because of all the contradictory directions they were receiving, till finally these last two bags too had to be left behind. It was early morning at the edge of some village where they had stopped to spend the night, and from not far away there came a heavy thud and then from the same direction a loud clicking. This was followed by a silence in which not knowing what to expect they did nothing at all, not having heard this particular sequence of sounds before, and then almost a minute later by a series of several small, powerful detonations. They went off simultaneously and in arbitrary directions, each explosion tight and self-contained, like a huge bag of marbles being emptied over a cement floor. Seeing at once that there would be no lull in which to reflect on the situation they gathered together their belongings and made for the main road. They had just joined the other families who were scrambling out of the area when underneath the noise of all the detonations and shouting another thud was heard in the distance, and then another click. They kept going then hearing a brief gasp behind him Dinesh turned around to see that his mother had collapsed on the ground a few meters away.

What happened immediately thereafter he could no longer recall. How he had felt at that moment and what he had done, whether he had screamed, or cried, or simply stood still, it was impossible to say. Perhaps everything had happened too fast for him to have paid any attention, or perhaps the moment had been blacked out subsequently by his memory, to save him from having to dwell on it in the future. Perhaps, at such times, a person's actions are determined solely by the unconscious movements of their arms and legs, by reactions that have never been reflected upon but which, unknown to the individual, have been preparing themselves quietly and meticulously in their muscles and nerves, so that when the moment comes they are executed without any thought or hesitation, and cannot therefore be remembered afterwards. Already by that point after all Dinesh had seen plenty of dead and injured bodies, strewn across the sides of roads, lying in the ruins of huts and houses. He'd always done his best to not get distracted, to keep his gaze locked ahead and to keep moving forward, but surely by then his eyes and ears had registered enough to know that in general, at such times, when bombs were falling everywhere and staying or slowing down could only mean death, there was no time to stop and grieve or to deal with the deceased in any reasonable way. Surely by then his body at least had become aware that you simply had to leave the dead behind at such times, sometimes even the injured, regardless of any misgivings you felt, if you were able at such times to feel anything at all.

All Dinesh could remember with any clarity was that some time later, perhaps a few minutes, perhaps half an hour, as he was running with both their bags in the same direction as everybody else, the detonations still going off all around him, it had occurred to him, all of a sudden, that there was something inappropriate about taking the bags with him while his mother was lying there unprotected on the ground. His legs weakened and he began to feel strangely weightless and exposed as he continued running, in the vicinity of his chest especially, as though his warm, living heart had been removed from the security of his rib cage and was lying back there on the ground, precariously beating on the dusty, windy, violent earth. His run slowed to a walk, then gradually to a stop. He stood there in the middle of the chaotic road for a moment, uncertain what he should do, then turned around and began running back, pushing past all the people who continued running the way he had come. The body was lying where he vaguely expected, a large dark featureless shape on the ground. He knew it was his mother without having to look and keeping his eyes well averted he pulled out a sari from one of the bags and draped it quickly over the body, so that all the flesh and skin was covered up, not a finger or a toe or a strand of hair visible. He placed the two bags carefully on either side of the stationary body and tucked the sari's edges firmly beneath them, so it wouldn't be blown away by the wind. Taking from the bags only what remained of their money, he stood up, and without looking back, began running again in the direction of the others. His chest felt strangely empty still but he was reassured somewhat by the thought that the bags beside his mother would protect her and provide her also with some identity. Before long they would probably be pilfered he knew, but it was comforting to think that for a while at least she would not be alone.

The only possessions Dinesh had carried since then were little objects that he found here and there and took pity on. A blue ballpoint that no longer wrote, a stainless steel cup, or an old yellow toothbrush with worn-away bristles, anything that was lost or abandoned by other evacuees and that seemed to him in need of companionship. He would pick them up and hold on to them for a while, let his fingers run up and down their surfaces lightly and carefully, the way a blind man might with an unknown object placed suddenly in his hands, usually only to leave them behind again, sometimes accidentally, sometimes intentionally, no more than a few days later. The object he'd held on to longest he found one day as he was walking along a deserted path between two small villages. There was something half-embedded in the red earth ahead of him, its visible surface plastered with soil except for a small section that gave out a mute glimmer. Stopping in front of it he crouched down and brushed a little at the dirt. The coating was hard so he wet his thumb with a little saliva and rubbed into the surface more vigorously, so that the dirt began to soften and the yellow metal beneath began to shine through. Moving his hands away he contemplated the thing for a while, tracing the ground around it respectfully with his fingers as if for some clue, but unable to guess what it could be he gave in at last to his urge to pull it out. It came out with a little loosening, a sculpted piece of solid brass the size of a child's fist, half a kilo maybe, maybe a little more. It looked like the handle of a door, though it was rounded like the wooden knobs on drawers rather than elongated like the plastic or iron handles usually on doors. Dinesh gazed at it silently for a while and then stood up with it and continued walking, wetting his fingertips with spit occasionally to polish off its surface, enjoying its weight as he shuttled it back and forth between his hands. For more than two weeks he took it with him wherever he went, dropping it into his shirt pocket when he needed the use of his hands and then at a quiet moment later, sometimes several hours afterwards, remembering it again with surprise, like a friend he forgot was waiting for him at home. Sitting or lying down he would press the cool heavy object to the hot skin of his face, hold it gently against his tired eyes, and listen to the beating of the blood vessels in his eyelids against the brass. He would squeeze it in his hands sometimes, as though to create a dent in the impenetrable surface, and was amazed each time by its solidity, by how strong and permanent it seemed. He grew more and more attached to the doorknob, and out of a slowly mounting fear that he would lose or be forced to abandon his companion, he decided at last to preempt the possibility by saying goodbye to it once and for all. He wrapped the doorknob carefully in a plastic bag one afternoon, dug a pit beside a tree where the earth was particularly soft, and tucked it into the ground so that it was cozily positioned. He covered up the hole, and with a little dejection continued on his way.

It was strange to think of that doorknob now, buried somewhere safely underground while he was above ground in a different place entirely. The path he'd traveled in the last months was littered though not only with the doorknob but also with all the other things he'd found, looked after briefly, and then left behind. He'd left behind a trail he could follow all the way back to his mother if he wanted, even though there was very little he could remember consciously about the way he'd come. It was as though a trace had been made of all his movements across the earth, a record of all the places he'd been and maybe even of what he had done, leading not only from where he was now to his mother but also, ultimately, back to his village where the evacuation had begun. Perhaps the trace would remain after he died, marking out the path he'd taken for all time, or perhaps, on reflection most likely in fact, it would soon disappear. Perhaps everything he'd found had been left by others who'd found them in various places before him, people who like him had looked after them a while before leaving them behind, and perhaps, if that was the case, they would be picked up again by those traveling behind him, to be deposited ultimately somewhere far from where he'd left them, like a seashell pushed further and further along the coast by the action of subsequent waves. It was impossible to say but maybe the objects he'd looked after had already been scattered, so that already no coherent line could be drawn from his mother and his home to him. Maybe his trail had been so thoroughly mingled with the trails of those who had come before and after that already it was impossible to distinguish his from theirs, and in a sense, therefore, him from them.

A murmur sounded from beside him, and Dinesh sat up straight. Ganga shifted slightly on the bed and turned so that instead of facing the rock she was lying supine, one arm draped across her chest and the other stretching away from her body. Dinesh stayed motionless for a moment, afraid any noise he made could wake her up, but Ganga kept still in her new position, and satisfied she was still fast asleep he let his body relax. How long he'd been sitting there in the darkness it was difficult to know. An hour maybe, maybe even longer, lost in thought, rocking back and forth unknowingly to the soft, regular rhythm of Ganga's breathing. All the while they had been next to each

other, she lying with her head on one side of the earthen pillow and
he sitting on the other, but entranced by the gentle and even sound of
her chest rising and falling, of air entering and leaving her body like
waves quietly advancing and receding, he'd forgotten it was a living
human he was listening to, and not just any living human but his wife.
He leaned down cautiously across the pillow and gazed at Ganga's
shadowed face. Her jaw was slightly unhinged and her expression was
slack, empty of all the tension that had held it stiff during the day. Her
lips were twitching faintly, with words that couldn't be made out, and
beneath her eyelids strange images seemed to flicker and die. She was
dreaming it seemed, floating or falling through some world that was
contained entirely inside her. What kind of world it was Dinesh didn't
know, needless to say, he had no access to what she was dreaming, but
the fact that such a place could be sustained inside her calm, still body
filled him nevertheless with a strange reverence.

It was difficult to know how Ganga felt about the marriage now,
whether she still had reservations, or whether having been around him
for some time now her feelings had changed. She'd been reluctant
about leaving her father's tent while she was preparing dinner, it was
true, but a change had come over her by the time they'd finished eating, and she had no longer seemed troubled by the thought of leaving
for the clearing. The anxiety that appeared on her face earlier had disappeared, and in contrast to their earlier impenetrability her features
seemed softer and less uncompromising, as though in the interim she'd
become more accepting of the marriage somehow. As though the move
was to be permanent rather than temporary she decided that they
would take not only the beige bag her father had given them, but also
the cooking utensils and the bags of rice and dhal. She even folded up
the tarpaulin sheet that had been laid out across the entrance of her

family's tent, leaving behind only the sari that had lain on top of it, and probably only so that the tent wouldn't seem abandoned when they left. When they had gathered everything together, she the pots, plates, food, and ladle, he the bag and rolled-up tarpaulin, she motioned to him to lead the way to the clearing, as though to be clear that it was because of him that she was leaving, and he leading the way they walked silently through the camp, taking care to be as discreet as possible. They moved together at the same pace without any conscious effort, raising their feet from the ground and moving them forward at the same time and with the same rhythm, neither one having to slow down or speed up for the other. When they came to the clearing they put the things down quietly, careful not to disturb the place's peace. Glancing at him briefly as if but not really for permission Ganga picked up the tarpaulin and unrolled it across the moist earth in front of the rock. She took out from near the top of the beige bag a sari that belonged either to her or her mother, folded it in two since it was too large for the bed, and then waving it up in the air so it billowed out like a real bedsheet, laid it out over the tarpaulin. She straightened out the bends and creases so the sari was spread out as smoothly as possible over the tarpaulin, then patted it down to make sure it was soft and dry. Placing her slippers neatly just beyond the border of the bed she yawned softly and lay down facing the rock. Dinesh had hoped the yawn was a way of communicating that they could lie down together rather than sit up, not that she was tired and wanted to rest, but before he could decide how to handle the situation her body had wrapped itself into a ball and he could hear the soft, regular breathing of her sleep.

Perhaps she had simply been tired. Perhaps she had been upset still about her father's disappearance, and simply wanted to lie down so that she could contemplate it alone. It was difficult to know with any certainty, but in any case he probably shouldn't read too much into it Dinesh knew. Now that she was asleep he finally had the opportunity to study her appearance without hindrance, and probably that would be a better measure of how she felt about the marriage than anything she'd actually said or done. Raising himself up as soundlessly as he could from his position against the rock, Dinesh leaned forward onto the balls of his feet. He shuffled sideways, half crouching, along the pebble-and-stone border of the bed, the ferns behind him lightly tickling his back, till he was halfway between Ganga's head and feet. He paused for a moment to make sure his movements hadn't disturbed her sleep, then leaning back a little he tried to take in the entirety of her existence all at once. Ganga was tall, but stretched out in front of the large rock that protected his home, her eyes closed and her face unknowing, she seemed small, vulnerable. The dress that rested silently over her body gleamed dully in the blue-black light, and beneath it the rising and falling of her chest and sunken waist seemed like a protest, like a slight but definite defiance of the world. Dinesh leaned forward onto his hands and inched towards her small, arched feet. Every so often her little toes would tense up and curl, on the right foot mainly but also the left, as though she were running somewhere in her dream, or standing barefoot somewhere trying to maintain a hold on the ground with her feet. The tendons that ran from her toes became discernible during these brief movements and then disappeared, but the light veins that wrapped around them remained visible as they rose up her foot, around her finely articulated ankles, and disappeared into her legs. Ganga's dress had ridden up a little while she slept and small portions of her shins were left uncovered, glowing mutely as though filled with life. Dinesh lowered his head over this section of bare skin and shifted his gaze over and around it, as if to find out whether the sheen was a product of the light and angle, or whether it was due to something inherent in the skin. His head suspended low over her body, the slightly pungent smell of her dress in his nose, he then moved up past Ganga's thighs, dwelling for a moment above her groin, to her waist, which rose and fell as she breathed in and out. Each time it sank he felt an urge to lay his head down in the vanishing hollow, as if in falling into the dip of her waist he could drop down into some other world, though obviously he didn't dare try. He didn't want to wake her up, not because she would open her eyes and find him there inappropriately close to her, but because he didn't want to disturb the delicate existence of a life-form so at ease. And as if he didn't trust himself to be so close to her body without touching it, he raised his head up, and tried to focus on her again from a distance.

Half-open across the bed, beside her waist, lay Ganga's right hand. Her thin fingers were partially bent, as though she was unsure whether to continue holding on to something or whether to let it go. Dinesh lowered his face down over this hand as though to nudge it with his nose, but without making contact he resumed again his passage along her body. He moved slowly and patiently from the tender little fingertips to the slender wrist, along the long peaceful arm, to the sleeves of the dress, skipping over her shoulder to her neckline, to the bumps of her collarbones and her bare neck. Running beside the yellow cord of her thaali was a vein that rose vividly along the side of her neck before disappearing beneath her jaw. Like the thousands of other blood vessels that must have been hidden deep beneath her skin, traveling from her heart to the other parts of her body and then back again, this vein too must have been responsible for supplying life to some specific part of Ganga's body, perhaps even her face. Like her fingers and toes her face was still disturbed from time to time by subtle movements in her lips, eyelids, and eyebrows, and perhaps it was this particular vein that was responsible for this life. Watching these movements Dinesh felt again an urge to touch Ganga, not necessarily to lie upon her and let himself fall into her, but merely to touch her face, for a moment, with the tips of his fingers. He wanted to stroke the underside of her jaw, or to caress her eyebrows, or to put his head side by side against hers so their temples touched lightly, anything that would allow him to feel the frail tremor of blood pulsing under the surface of her skin, so that by listening to its soft beat he might permeate her dream. It was possible of course that her skin would feel different from what he hoped, coarse and lifeless like a stick or branch, or cool and grainy like a pebble or stone, but he was willing to take the risk in order to know what her skin really felt like, whether it was as warm as its glow made it seem or cold, whether he'd be able to sense any signs of life existing beneath or not. Holding back his breath he moved his face down closer to Ganga's, so they were almost though not quite touching, so he could smell the odor of her skin moist from light perspiration, and feel on his eyelids the light push and pressure of warm air expelled and cool air inhaled through her finely shaped nostrils. He would not only have touched her but would also have wrapped her in his arms if he could, squeezed her so hard that they collapsed into each other, but Ganga was alive he knew and she was whole, like other life-forms she was a fragile thing, and even the lightest touch could affect her.

A breeze swept through the trees, and the leaves around them stirred gently then settled. Dinesh leaned back. Ganga shifted obliviously and continued sleeping, the effect of his brief nearness absorbed without difficulty apparently into some aspect or other of her dream.

In a sense it was good that she'd been able to fall asleep. It meant she'd come to feel safe and comfortable in the clearing, that she'd found it in some way at least adequate to her needs. It was hard in fact not to feel a slight pride in his home, looking at her and how peacefully she slept, as well as at all the things she had brought, the plastic sheet and sari spread out neatly over the bed, the beige bag with all her belongings on its far border, and the cooking items piled casually on the ground beside it. All these new things made the clearing feel more concrete somehow, more substantial than before, as though its worth as a home had been objectively confirmed by how harmoniously these new elements fit in, by how natural they all seemed in their new places. Dinesh looked at Ganga to make sure she was still calmly asleep, then shuffled cautiously along the border of the bed to where the bag was, and gazed at it for a while motionlessly. In spite of the long traveling and hard conditions its tough canvas fabric still retained its robustness. Its seams still held its sides tightly together, and its zipper still fastened to keep its contents perfectly sealed. There was no doubt the bag had been opened and closed many times since it was packed for the first evacuation, and probably its contents had changed dramatically over the course of the journey, but all the same everything it contained Dinesh felt must still have belonged to the world in which Ganga had lived before the fighting began. If he opened it he would have a chance to glimpse this world somehow, inaccessible to him and most likely even to her now, and by doing so perhaps he would be able to understand a little better who Ganga was. It was with the same hope that in the tent earlier he had studied the bag's surface so meticulously with his hands, but now that that they were alone and Ganga was asleep he had the opportunity to go through each thing in the bag one by one, patiently and with understanding. Opening the bag and looking inside would be very different of course from merely caressing its surfaces. No other trace was left now of that world in which Ganga had lived, and by opening the bag there was a chance he could taint these last remaining vestiges, like an old photograph that is taken out of a grimy album so it can be examined more clearly, only to disintegrate at once. Dinesh looked again at Ganga, who was sleeping peacefully behind him still. Perhaps he would open the bag just to see what was on top, without actually looking through what was inside or taking anything out. He hesitated for a moment, then careful not to make too much noise, unzipped the bag. He parted the two edges, and leaned in close so he could see in the darkness.

Along the top of the bag there was an almost uniform layer of neatly folded clothes, saris mainly but also other clothing that Dinesh couldn't identify by the fabric, dresses probably and blouses. Tucked into one of the sides was the framed Lakshmi that Ganga's father had used for the marriage, and next to it the two cardboard folders that he'd pulled out in order to get to it. Without removing either of the folders he pried them open a little to see what he could of what was inside. There were documents, letters, and envelopes mainly, their edges crimped from having gotten wet at some point and their writing difficult to make out in the darkness. Opposite the folders were several neatly tied polythene bags, which he didn't want to touch for fear of the crinkling noise they would make, and at the far end of the bag where there were no clothes at all were the two water bottles that Ganga had filled before they had left, and packed neatly below them the two bags of rice and dhal. Dinesh leafed through a few of the clothes in the bag's center carefully, then let them fall back to their original positions. He couldn't see what was beneath them without actually pulling the clothes out, but he didn't want to insinuate his hands further into the bag. To probe into what was in the bottom of the bag rather than restrict himself to its topmost layers would be to needlessly expose the things it was protecting he felt, as if in order to learn Ganga's thoughts and feelings he were to make an incision in the back of her head, peel apart the outer layers of gray matter, and peer into the center. The things in the bag would be taken out whenever they were needed. There wasn't any hurry to find out what they were, for in time he would get to see everything that was there.

Dinesh quietly zipped the opening back shut, and sat for a while looking at the sealed bag, as though to ensure it looked the same as before he'd touched it, that it hadn't changed in any lasting way. He was about to get up to return to his seat when he noticed, on one side of the bag, an outer pocket. There were things inside he could tell from the way it bulged, though being a side pocket it couldn't have been anything of value, nothing he need fear tarnishing. He glanced back quickly to make sure Ganga was still sleeping, then leaned forward and unzipped the pocket, put his hand inside and felt around. The first thing he found, he could tell by its rounded corners and smooth polished surface, was a bar of soap, relatively unused. It was difficult to say what color it was in the darkness, light pink or yellow, but when he brought it to his nose and breathed in he recognized the sweet lime smell that had hovered around Ganga's skin earlier, when crouching down in front of her he'd tied the thaali around her neck. He put the soap in his shirt pocket and thrust his hand again into the bag's side pouch. The next thing his fingers distinguished was a rectangular strip of plastic, with a row of teeth extending evenly on one side, a comb it seemed like. He reached again into the pocket to identify the remaining items—a toothbrush, a few packets of toothpaste, and a slightly rusted pair of scissors—then put them back into the pocket and zipped it shut, satisfied for the moment with the soap and the comb.

Dinesh inched back to his position on the other side of the earthen pillow and sat down against the rock. He was still for a moment, but Ganga's soft breathing continued steadily beside him, completely undisturbed. He took the comb out of his pocket, looked at it for a while, then ran a fingertip across the row of teeth and listened to the pleasant sound they made as they sprang back upright. Slowly at first, then a few times more quickly, he drew the comb across his forearm. The points of the teeth touched his skin sharply through the layer of dirt and dead matter that had accumulated over his body, sent a refreshing shiver along his neck and back as each tooth took a distinct path simultaneously across his arm. Bringing it down to his legs then he drew the comb along the side of his calf, let the longer curlier hair of his legs be pulled up and stretched out so he could feel little pinpricks all over the skin. He continued for a while, first with the left leg then with the right, and then, realizing that the comb he was holding was the same comb he had seen Ganga using in the camp, that it was meant to be used on the hair of his head rather than the hair of his arms and legs, he raised it up and inserting it into his long unwashed, uncut hair, tried to draw the comb back across his head. He repeated the action at several different starting points, but though the teeth dug gently into his scalp and tickled pleasantly, his hair was too knotted and tangled for it to be properly combed. It had congealed into thick, oily clumps, cemented by the flakes of dandruff that fell down in front of him whenever he scratched his head, and wouldn't allow the comb past.

Dinesh lowered the comb again to his line of sight and gazed at it in the darkness. He ran his fingertip again across the row of teeth and listened as they sprang back. He felt the urge, suddenly, to wash himself. It had been so long since he'd last bathed, and using Ganga's bar of soap he could clean himself thoroughly now, not just his face but also his hair and his body. In the past few months he had done nothing more than dash a little water on his face from time to time, and neither that nor the rain that he sometimes got caught in had been sufficient to keep him clean. A stubborn film of salt, dust, and grease had formed all over his skin, caking his limbs and preventing full freedom of movement. His face had stiffened into a mask, making it impossible to express emotion, and the soles of his feet had been stained ochre so deeply by the clay that there was hardly any sensation in them at all, not even under the arches that used to be so ticklish when he was young. If he bathed now he could take his time scrubbing off all these lifeless extraneous layers, he could make his body light and free, return his skin to its former sensitivity. There was a chance too that by washing himself he could make himself more acceptable to Ganga, make her less ambivalent about their marriage. She was distant from him for other reasons too obviously, she was still affected by the death of her mother and brother and the desertion of her father, but maybe if he was clean and smelled good she would see him in a different way, as someone worthy of marrying rather than something to be ashamed of. There was a well he knew where in addition to bathing he'd be able to wash his sarong and shirt, scrub out the blood and grime, so that he could be in unsoiled clothes too. If he was clean and wore clean clothes maybe Ganga would come to see him as someone responsible, as someone reliable whom she could therefore trust. It was hard to say for sure but maybe if he scrubbed himself properly and used the soap generously she would find it easier to be close to him also, be more willing to let him lie down beside her, and perhaps even to hold her.

And though it was absurd for him to consider, since perhaps it wasn't possible for her to feel such things in her present state at all, perhaps she would even think he was handsome, if he bathed.

There was of course some risk in leaving the clearing at night. There was a chance he would be seen by the cadres, for he'd be more conspicuous now than in the daytime, especially since the other evacuees would no longer be up and about. It would take time moreover to walk to the well and back, and there was a danger that the shelling could begin while he was away. Usually when the camp was shelled at night it happened either just when darkness had fallen, at dinnertime or just before, or else right at the end, in the very early morning. There was a good chance that there would still be a few hours before the next episode started therefore, that no harm would come to Ganga if he left now for just a little while, though naturally there was also no guarantee, since when and where shells were dropped ultimately depended only on the mood of whoever was in charge in the army. Even if there was no shelling there was always the possibility that Ganga would wake up of her own accord. If that happened she would find that he had gone and be scared or worried, and perhaps even feel betrayed or abandoned. Dinesh glanced quickly at Ganga, who still seemed fast asleep. He could be back in less than forty-five minutes if he hurried, an hour at the most. The rice and dhal he'd eaten earlier was beginning to digest and he felt full of energy, able to accomplish anything. No sooner would he leave the clearing to get to the well than he would already be standing there he felt, the cool fresh water splashing over his tired, grimy body. The border of pebbles and stones he'd built around the bed would keep the area secure in the meantime, and nothing dangerous could possibly enter its perimeter while Ganga was still inside.

Dinesh got to his feet and moved to the bag, put the comb back into the side pocket and on a whim took out the pair of scissors, which he could use if he felt like it to cut his hair. Straightening up he took a few long, loping steps over the ferns and shrubs to the edge of the clearing, then stopped and hesitated. He turned back to look at Ganga once more. She was lying there on the bed with arms outstretched, still calm and unknowing. In a strange way it would be pleasant to leave and then return, Dinesh felt, to come back and find her still lying there, safely and peacefully, breathing slowly in and out beside the rock. Just as coming home from school or work in the past he would notice certain small, inconspicuous changes around the house, that there was now a letter on the table, that the windows had been opened or shut, or that wet clothes were hanging on the clothesline, and feel reassured somehow by these signs that his life was part of something larger that had its own momentum and energy, something with its own separate impulse for movement, in the same way it would be gratifying to return to the clearing after his bath and find that Ganga had gone on existing there without him, that independently of him her small chest had continued rising and falling, that the faint vessels beneath her skin had continued their delicate pulsing. Comforted by this thought he turned and made his way through the trees.

5

DINESH MOVED QUICKLY at first through the darkness of the canopy, in spite of being unable to see the ground in front of him. It felt pleasant to use his legs vigorously after having sat down for so long, to feel the pressure in his feet and the strain in his calves as they lifted up the weight of his body with each step. He moved surely and without hesitation along his habitual path, and then as the trees gradually thinned and the darkness let up he found himself slowing down, not so much from fatigue as from a kind of nervousness about what would happen on his way through the camp. His movement became more tentative, and then finally, at the edge of the jungle, he came to a stop. The sky, immense and empty, opened out over him. The half-moon was brightly visible, except for brief interludes in which whorls of translucent cloud passed beneath, and it gave out a soft blue backlight that seemed wholly without source. Stretching out in front of him each tent in the vast settlement absorbed and reflected this light, like a nighttime gathering of wraiths with nowhere to hide. The dull thudding of artillery and gunfire could be heard in the distance, but the camp itself felt cocooned in silence, as though the fighting that was raging on nonstop to the north, west, and south was a blanket in which the camp was swaddled rather than something that could enter and destroy it at will, without warning, many times a day.

Careful not to disturb the pervasive stillness, Dinesh began walking quietly through the periphery of the camp. Most of the evacuees were inside their tents, together with their families and things, but many were sleeping under the open sky, on the ground and in uncovered trenches, individually and in groups of up to four or five. Observing them as he passed into the more populated sections of the camp Dinesh found himself filled, slowly, with the sacredness of being awake in a place in which everybody else was asleep. Those who had just fallen asleep he could tell apart easily, by their furrowed brows and curled lips, by the effort and struggle to block out the world that was imprinted still on their faces. Their muscles were taut, their bodies curled into tight balls, their closed eyes screwed up as if to prevent anything outside them from entering in, fighting to obtain or retain a state of sleep before it was made impossible by the next shelling in a way that was not so different, perhaps, from how long ago, if he woke up earlier than necessary in the morning, he would refuse to open his eyes and stubbornly pretend to still be sleeping, despite knowing full well that soon he'd have to get up and rejoin the world. The people who had been asleep longer, in contrast, let their bodies relax and their lips droop. Their faces were peaceful and unstrained, and no longer displayed any sign of a struggle to fend off the world. Most still had their bags under their heads like pillows, or their arms and legs slung around them like teddy bears, but they were no longer clutching them like the others or even holding on to them. They seemed to have mostly lost concern with the world immediately outside them, as though their gaze had turned more or less inwards, away from their eyes and ears and hands and feet. Most of them were dreaming, their lips twitching and their eyelids flickering like Ganga's had in the clearing, their fingers and toes curling and uncurling, suspended in an uncertain realm of shifting things and obscure feelings, partly within the world still but mostly not, while a few of them, it seemed, had managed to let go fully. Their mouths open and their arms and legs sprawled out, the rising and falling of the chests so subtle it was hard to tell if they were still breathing, a small but increasing number had entirely ceased dreaming, it seemed, had become lost in a deeper, more timeless sleep. It was as though these sleepers had disengaged themselves from the world entirely, from not only its objects but also from the forms through which in ordinary life these objects were perceived, as though they had left their bodies lying unguarded in the camp and gone off to some other place, trusting meanwhile that they would be safe though in fact of course shards of metal could come raining down from the sky at any time.

It was these people especially, lost in this deeper, fuller sleep, that Dinesh did not want to disturb. He took care to avoid stepping too close to their heads as he moved, and looking at their calm, unknowing faces as he passed he sensed acutely how his body slowed down beside them, how carefully his feet arched and lowered themselves onto the earth, how silently his calves tensed as they lifted his body and shifted its weight onto the next foot. No sound he made would wake them up probably, but he was fearful of disturbing the silence that surrounded their sleep all the same, wary in the same way that upon entering an empty temple one was wary of making the slightest sound, as if in a sense there was no real difference between the silence demanded by the divine and the silence demanded by the sleep of other humans. It was as though having relinquished totally the world outside them these sleepers were in the presence now of something special, of something elusive and beautiful that had appeared or become visible inside them and which completely ensnared them, as when one peers into the bottom of a well that is momentarily unused, in which the movement of water has calmed and even the gentlest ripples on the surface have stilled, and looking down one can see the things that have remained silently unnoticed at the very bottom all the long years of its use. Unable to pull away one was drawn closer and closer inside, and just as even an insect skating lightly across the water's surface might suffice to call back one's attention from the depths, make one blink and turn away, Dinesh was afraid that even the slightest movement he made might take those people lost deep in sleep away from what they had found.

Walking by all the people sleeping in the camp Dinesh wondered whether perhaps he had been mistaken to not try harder to fall asleep in these last months, not merely because he was tired, but because perhaps in not sleeping he was missing out on something that he would not again have the chance to savor. For so many years he had tried to avoid sleep, to fend it off as yet another distraction from the central purpose of life, a purpose he could never identify but which he waited for nevertheless with yearning, hoping it would somehow show itself in the night sky. Even when he was tired and had to be up early he would stay up late, as if by staying up he was putting himself in position to have some long-awaited experience that life would not bestow if he fell asleep. Perhaps though this attitude had been mistaken, perhaps he should have been more willing to fall asleep in the past, perhaps he should have been more sensitive to what sleep could give, to what it

gave everybody now. When you were asleep you always hated distur-
bances after all, when you were asleep you were always happy to stay
that way for the rest of your life. Even now he was refusing to go to
bed, refusing to sleep as if in staying awake something would happen
to justify the difficulty of having stayed awake and struggled so long,
though what reward could possibly be forthcoming, what good
could possibly come of being awake now? He had wanted to bathe
so that Ganga would accept him, but even if it helped he would still
have to wait till she woke for her to notice, and he might just as well
have tried to sleep now and bathe in the morning instead, at least
then he could have let her know before leaving her all alone. If he
wanted of course he could still go back, Ganga would still be quietly
sleeping in the clearing, probably by now she would be lost deeply in
sleep. He could go back and fall asleep beside her still, he could curl
up his body and put his hands under his head and drop bit by bit into
that deep, unknowing state himself. If he went back and lay down beside Ganga he could have all that, he knew, but he had come so far
now, he was almost at the well. It would be good to clean his body he
knew, and it would be nicer to fall asleep once he was clean. He wanted,
for the time being at least, to stay awake.

The well he had planned to use was just behind the school buildings that housed the clinic, in a small backyard circumscribed by a
patch of jungle to the south and west. As he approached the area Dinesh
took the long way around, so he could avoid walking past the dozens
of wounded evacuees who had been laid out on tarpaulins immediately in front of the clinic. Their bodies were thin and slit and ruptured, separated only by little strips of bloodstained ground, and he
would rather avoid being in their proximity if he could. He still had to
pass the many unclaimed bodies that had been laid out to the southeast

of the clinic, though, and as he drew near them Dinesh became increasingly anxious about stepping on something dead. He took long,
cautious steps and let only the front of his feet come into contact with
the ground, so that he was walking more or less on tiptoe. If he stepped
on anything that was soft but that seemed to have structure he would
immediately stop, his body temporarily frozen, then nudging the object fearfully with the edge of his slippers would try to verify that it
was just some normal, natural thing, a large plant or a twig under a
pile of leaves. He had become accustomed it was true to lifeless bodies and body parts over the course of all the fighting, it wasn't something that had bothered him greatly for a long time, but something
about having been so near all the people sleeping in the camp, and also
to Ganga's quiet, delicately alive body in the clearing, made him anxious about being around them now. There were other pumps and wells
in the camp that he might have used instead, but the problem was that
they couldn't provide any privacy. Bathing at the other wells or pumps
meant being in plain sight of the other evacuees and potentially also
the movement's patrols. The area of the camp near the clinic on the
other hand was for some reason usually avoided by the cadres, and the
clinic well itself was perfectly enclosed between the back of the school
buildings and the encircling brush and trees. None of the injured were
kept near the well, and the only people who ever went there were
nurses and volunteers who filled up buckets of water to clean wounds,
wash instruments, and give to the injured, some of whom, especially
those who'd been struck around the stomach, were insatiably thirsty.
There was a chance one of them could be using the well now, but it
was close to midnight, they were in that brief three- or four-hour span
in which almost everybody in the camp was trying to sleep, even in
the clinic, and the area therefore would most likely be unoccupied.

Dinesh shuffled through the narrow path between the outside wall of the staff room and the trees, the leaves brushing his face in the darkness till arriving at the corner of the building he stood completely still, and surveyed the school's backyard. In its center the thick, circular wall of the well could be seen, three or four feet high, around it only bare earth, dotted here and there with patches of grass glowing dully in the moonlight. Nestled between the back walls of the two school buildings on one side and the ring of trees that formed the jungle's boundary on the other, the area seemed strangely calm and peaceful. Except for the bucket beside the well and two stretchers improvised from sticks and sarongs that were lying on the ground, there was no sign that it had been visited by humans in many years. Dinesh stayed hidden behind the corner of the staff room for a minute or two longer, and only when he felt sure that nobody was around did he begin moving across the open yard towards the far side of the well. He tried to hush the sound of his heartbeat as he walked, as if by being silent he could compensate for the conspicuousness of his movements, and when he stepped up on the slightly raised concrete platform he stood perfectly motionless beside the wall of the well, as if to convince anybody watching that he was really just an inanimate object. Soundlessly he removed his slippers and lowered himself down, so that he was sitting cross-legged, his back against the smoothly cemented wall. A short distance before him the tangle of brush began, thickening for a few feet before becoming indistinguishable from the trees, and enclosed by the two buildings behind him and the semicircle of jungle in front of him and to his sides, he felt screened and barricaded from all directions, suitably protected. Nobody would be able to see him unless they came right up to the well, and if he didn't make any noise nobody would have any reason to. He was sufficiently alone and enclosed he felt, not permanently or impenetrably, but enough at least to make himself vulnerable for a short period of time.

Dinesh took out of his shirt pocket the bar of soap and the pair of scissors that he'd taken from Ganga's bag. He'd picked up an old newspaper that he noticed on the ground while walking through the camp, and unfolding one of the sheets he spread it out on the concrete before him and placed the soap over its center to weigh it down. Taking the scissors in his right hand and plucking out a lengthy tuft of hair from the top of his head with his left, he hesitated for a moment, as if he was about to do something of significance, then snipped it off. He cut more off the crown, moved to the hair on the back of his head, then jumped to the front, depositing each of the cut tufts carefully on the newspaper. The scissor blades were slightly rusted and his thumb snagged uncomfortably in the small lower handle, but the cutting itself was easy because of the way his hair had congealed into discrete oily clumps. Both shoulders began to ache slightly from the strain of keeping his arms elevated but he continued patiently along the sides, carefully around his ears, and then again to the back of his head, down to his neck. He kept going till all over his head his hair felt of roughly the same length, no more than an inch or so long, then put the scissors down and let his arms fall to his sides. On the newspaper in front of him lay a large creature-like mound of black hair, more than enough to cover the scalp of someone who'd gone bald. It was hard to believe he'd carried so much on his head for so long, and that despite its volume he'd hardly been able to feel its weight. He removed the bar of soap and swept all the individual strands and clumps from the edges of the newspaper into its center. Cupping the mound so it stayed in place he leaned forward and submerged the tip of his nose into its peak. He breathed in deeply, as if through its scent he could glean the significance of what he'd removed from his body, of all that had happened during the period in which what he'd cut had grown, but his hair smelled, despite how deeply he inhaled, of nothing.

Dinesh leaned back up against the wall and for a moment was still. He looked at his thumb, which was hurting still from holding the scissors, and noticed for the first time the state of his fingernails. For most of the evacuation he'd bitten them, more in order to have something to do than out of a desire to keep himself presentable, but though the biting had slowed the lengthening of his nails it had not stopped it altogether. They had grown now to almost half an inch long, almost as long on his toes as well, and their undersides were encrusted with thick, black-brown grime. He tried scraping at the dirt under the nail of his left index finger with the thumb of his opposite hand, but the dirt was far too densely packed to be removed this way. Picking up the scissors again he brought his left index finger close to his face, and tried to cut the nail. He took care to work the scissor slowly around the curve of the fingertip, so that the nail came off all at once and without shooting away, then deposited the clipping in a corner of the newspaper and began to work on the next finger. When he was ten or maybe eleven years old his father had once smacked him hard, he remembered, for cutting his nails after dark. He had been told he shouldn't once before that, that if it was past six o'clock he should wait until the next morning, but his father hadn't seemed so angry that first time, perhaps because he hadn't actually started to cut his nails. This second time he was ordered to get on his knees and search the floor till all twenty clippings were found, and once gathered his father had taken them to the uncultivated area behind their house and flung them as far as he could into the brush. Where the rule had come from and what its rationale had been he hadn't known, but after that it had never been transgressed. His first instinct thereafter had been to check what time of day it was each time he felt the urge to cut his nails, and the practice had remained even after his father died two years after the event. Today, however, he'd remembered the rule only once he'd already started cutting his nails, as if the memory of his father, who he was thinking of now for the first time in so long, was so far away that even his firmest injunctions no longer influenced him. It wasn't too late yet to stop cutting of course, he'd not even completed his left hand, but now that he'd started there was no point in stopping Dinesh felt, since the rule had already been broken. Even if he could save himself from its consequences by disposing of the nails in the appropriate way, as his father had done, he wasn't quite sure how to do so, whether he would have to move them away from the place they'd been cut, whether what mattered was that they were put in a place where other people wouldn't see or step on them, or whether it was fine so long as they didn't remain in one's home. In any case he wasn't sure he wanted to get rid of his nails at all, for there would be something satisfying about packing them away carefully with his hair. Maybe the prohibition on cutting nails after dark lasted only until midnight. After midnight a new day began after all, in a sense in fact it was already morning, and maybe therefore the rule hadn't even been violated.

When Dinesh was done with his left hand he switched to the right, moving from the thumb to the little finger, then uncrossing his legs he started on his thicker and more stubborn toenails, first on the right foot, then on the left. When all his fingernails and toenails had been cut he gathered them up from the newspaper into the palm of his hand, brought them to his nose, and breathed in their intimate and slightly nauseating scent. They contained in them the accumulation of all the different places he had walked and all the different things he had held in the last couple of months, and unlike his scentless hair they gave off a vivid account of his recent past. Dinesh breathed them in several times deeply, to take in all they contained and to memorize their scent, then lifted the mound of hair a little up off the newspaper and tucked the fingernail clippings inside, so they were hidden underneath the hair. Holding down the mound with one hand he slowly drew one corner of the sheet of newspaper across it with the other. He folded the corner down over the mound and drew the opposite corner over the first, then did the same for the opposite diagonal, creating a little package out of the newspaper. He creased its sides tightly so it wouldn't unfold, so that it looked like one of the little packets of ash given out at big temples for devotees to take back home, then placed it down carefully on the ground in front of him. He stared at the package of dead bodily matter for a while, and seeing all of it so neatly and tightly packaged he felt somehow invigorated, as if the elimination of his hair and nails had freed him of some burden, heightening briefly his sense of being alive.

A sudden tiredness followed on the heels of this momentary invigoration, first washing over Dinesh like an unexpected wave and then almost drowning him. His eyelids began to feel heavy, his head light. As though he'd become unburdened of his bond to the world by the cutting of his hair and nails, he felt ready all at once to fall asleep. If he stayed sitting down there was a chance he could do so accidentally he knew, and since with Ganga alone in the clearing he couldn't take a chance, gritting his teeth he stood up. The sudden upward movement made him feel even more lightheaded, and he held on to the well wall till he regained his equilibrium. There was still some water in the steel bucket that lay with its rope uncoiled by the base of the well, and cupping it in his hands he doused his face with it.

The water felt good on his burning eyes, and somewhat refreshed, he leaned upon the wall and looked down into the hollow. The well was fairly wide, two full meters in diameter, but was too deep for the moonlight to fall all the way to the bottom. The water could be told apart from the lower reaches of the walls only by the dark glimmer it gave off, and beneath this polished, unbroken surface Dinesh could feel the strong pull of the silence and stillness it contained. Not taking his eyes off the water he groped for the steel bucket beside him. He was reluctant to disturb the water's surface but began lowering the bucket down anyway, careful not to let it hit the wall as it descended. The rope slipped slowly through his hands, one giving way to the other in turns, lower and lower till at last the sound of the steel hitting the water echoed up from below. Jerking the rope about so that the bucket tipped sideways into the water he waited as it filled, then pulled it heavily out of the well, up over the rim, onto the concrete platform beside him. He had planned to take off his clothes and wash them first, rather than keeping them on and letting them get wet as he bathed, for only if he washed them separately would he be able to soap them properly and let them soak. In what order to wash them though he wasn't sure, whether to do his shirt first and then his sarong, his sarong first and then his shirt, or whether to simply do them both at once. He was a little nervous of being fully naked and so perhaps he could wash just his shirt first, and then when he felt more comfortable the sarong. He could bathe afterwards, when he'd been in the area for a while and felt assured that no one would enter suddenly and find him there.

Crouching down slowly before the bucket he unbuttoned his shirt, starting at the collar then moving downwards, then peeled it off his back and dipped it into the surface. The water remained clear for a moment, and then as the shirt was drenched and became heavy in the water a cloudy, clayey suspension began to emerge. Dinesh massaged the cotton fabric, kneaded it between his thumbs and forefingers so that everything that had accumulated there was rubbed out and dissolved, all the dried sweat, and dust, and blood. There still was plenty of space inside the bucket, and less nervous now that he was crouching down again, he slipped out of his sarong and underwear, compressed them into a ball, and dropped them too into the water. Completely naked he leaned forward onto the balls of his feet and scrubbed, stretched, and squeezed the three articles, did his best to wrench from them all the grime that had gathered in their interstices and made them thick and stiff. He could no longer remember where the blue-and-green-checked sarong had come from, how long he'd had it or whether it had been bought or gifted. The striped white shirt had been given to him on some special occasion years ago he vaguely knew, Deepavali most probably, though how old he'd been and what had happened that day he was not able to say. He lifted the shirt out of the murky water and pressed a part of the fabric gently between both his hands, as if by letting his palms meet through the tiny gaps in the stitching he would be able to remember its history more clearly. He closed his eyes and did his best to clear his mind. Furrowing his brows, he tried to concentrate. The details were there somewhere, he knew, but nothing came back to him, neither sounds, images, nor smells. He could sense the presence of that time in the past as if it were floating just beyond the edge of his consciousness but was unable to touch it, like a person standing outstretched on a ladder striving to grasp a feather swaying playfully just out of reach who feels, all the more vividly, nothing but the rung around which their toes are curled, and the strain in their fingertips and arms. No matter how hard he tried to remember the origin of the shirt all Dinesh could feel was his body and the things it was in immediate contact with, the water in which his hands were immersed, the wet concrete beneath his feet, and the air whose constant movement in and out of him raised and lowered his chest.

Dinesh took the shirt and sarong out of the bucket and hung them across the wall of the well, tipped the bucket over and watched as the thick brown water emptied out and seeped into the ground. He stood up and lowered the bucket into the well once more, waited impatiently in his nudity as it filled, then heaved it up and crouched back down. He took the bar of soap and started working it vigorously into the shirt, rubbing the parts of the fabric that he soaped with the unsoaped parts so that the suds were spread out evenly. He did the same for the sarong and the underwear and when all three items were fully lathered he immersed them in the new water, watching as a suspension emerged again out of the water's clarity, cloudier this time but less dirty than before. In a way it wasn't surprising of course that he could remember nothing of the origins of his clothes. It was only because of the proposal that morning and the marriage in the afternoon, after all, that he'd begun to dwell on what had happened in the last months at all, to recollect to some degree everything that had happened since they had evacuated their home. For so long he'd moved about in a state of stupefaction, devoid of memory, thought, and perception, like a tortoise with its head and limbs retracted fully into its shell, so how could it be surprising if he couldn't understand anything of what had happened even further back in time? Recollections of that life did come back to him now and then, but only in brief traces, in silent images that came of their own accord, that could not be connected with other things, and that were gone before he had time to recognize them. They left

behind only a vague sense of vacancy, like a childhood home one re-
turns to years later and finds emptied of all its contents, only nails remaining where pictures were once hung, and lighter-colored sections
of floor where furniture once was. If someone asked him specific questions about the past he would probably have been able to respond, it
was true. He would have been able to recite where he had lived, the
exact village and lane, to describe the members of his family, what he
had studied at school, and how he had spent his free time. No matter
how accurately he responded to these questions, though, his answers
would have been hollow. He could no longer remember the faces of
his mother, father, or brother, could no longer remember anything of
the routine of their lives or the mood in which they had lived, and anything he said about that time would have been devoid of substance,
like black-and-white outlines in a children's coloring book. All he was
really in a position to understand at that moment were the ten or eleven
months since the evacuation had begun, just as all he could really hope
or plan for was restricted to the few hours left in each day, and perhaps, in an amorphous way, the few days or weeks before that abstract
point at which he too would be killed. From the hemisphere of his mind
devoted to the past and the hemisphere devoted to the future great
swathes had been shaved off, and enclosing the sensitive little core that
belonged to the present there remained only the thin layer of the recent past and near future, leaving him without that recourse to the distant past or future by which in times of difficulty ordinary people
were able to ignore or endure or at least justify the present moment.

In one of their early displacements Dinesh and his mother had set
up camp next to a woman whose son had been killed in the war effort
a year before, back before the evacuation had begun. She had come
with her husband and her twelve-year-old daughter, and spent most

of her free time reading her Bible inside their tent, rocking back and forth as she intoned the words in a low whisper. She couldn't have been that old, no more than her early forties at most probably, but her hair was graying and her cheeks were withered, her eyes submerged in a fluid that constantly seemed on the verge of dripping. She seemed somewhat agitated at first, Dinesh noticed, in his presence. She would stare at him when she thought he wasn't looking, and from time to time made impulsive movements in his direction that she had to struggle greatly to subdue, as if her body was confusing him for someone else and the mistake could only be prevented by great mental exertion. For two weeks Dinesh and his mother shared a dugout with the woman and her family, and as the discord inside her lessened and she became more comfortable around him she began sometimes to speak to him of her son, as if he and Dinesh were first cousins who had never had the chance to meet. He would have been his same age if he were alive, she told him, and the two of them were about the same height. Dinesh was maybe just a little bit taller, though her son was a few shades fairer and better built. He was one of the best netball players in his school, and though his marks weren't the best he studied as hard as he could too. He would do anything she asked him to do, and sometimes even before she asked, as though no sooner was a thought formed in her mind than he would begin to act on it. In his last few months at home he became irritable, the woman told Dinesh, shifting her voice to a lower register, as if letting him in on a secret. In that period when the movement was combing all the villages for young people to recruit he would argue with his father and sometimes even shout. It was only natural of course that he would get upset when they had to stop him from going to school and seeing his friends, when he was forced to stay inside the house all day so as not to be seen and taken away. When the recruiters came to the village they would hide him in an old oil drum buried in the garden, leaving him smothered inside the hot ground for hours on end. Each time it happened he got more resentful, and when finally out of sheer frustration he decided to give up hiding and join the movement he didn't even say good-bye to them, he just left one night without a word, as though it was the movement and not his family who had his best interests at heart. The woman had been looking at the ground, squinting as if she were looking into the distance, but then she looked up at Dinesh and smiled wistfully. His body had come back lifeless it was true, but her son was still alive somewhere she felt. He was alive and healthy in a higher world she knew, she could feel it, he was alive somewhere, she was sure.

At the time Dinesh had simply nodded, as if to let the woman know that he too agreed this was a reasonable belief. Despite the conviction with which she'd spoken he had been unable to feel anything but sorry for her, for like the countless others in her situation who couldn't acknowledge all that they had lost, she too was probably only saying what she needed in order to survive. Perhaps he had been mistaken, though, to dismiss her so quickly, perhaps he'd been too condescending in his reaction to her. Perhaps there'd been some truth in what the woman said, which he just hadn't been in a position to see. Being close to someone meant more than being next to them after all, it meant more than simply having spent a lot of time with them. Being close to someone meant the entire rhythm of that person's life was synchronized with yours, it meant that each body had learned how to respond to the other instinctually, to its gestures and mannerisms, to the subtle changes in the cadence of its speech and gait, so that all the movements of one person had gradually come to be in subconscious harmony with those of the other. Two people truly close to each other were two bodies fully in tune with each other, each able to respond to the other in any kind of situation without thinking, and because this knowledge was imprinted above all in the memory of the nerves and muscles, in the hands and feet, in the cheeks, lips, and eyelids, perhaps it made sense what the woman said, perhaps it was even true. In saying that her son was alive still all she meant was that she retained this knowledge even after her son had died, that it was engrained in her motor system, was alive inside her and ready at any moment to spring into action, so that if more than a year after his death her son were to suddenly stroll up to the tent where she was making tea she would smile at him first and begin pouring him his cup and only afterwards freeze and in dread or disbelief wonder how her dead son had come to be standing before her. Just as another person might in the same kind of situation say that a part of themselves was dead, though physically they were perfectly intact, meaning only that a person around which an entire aspect of their lives had grown and entwined had been taken away, leaving this part of themselves to go limp or atrophy, all the woman meant was that though her son's heart was no longer beating she still carried the rhythm of his life inside her muscles and nerves, and that in a sense therefore he was still alive and well inside her own body, just as he had been before he was born. Why people responded differently in such cases was difficult to say, but in any case what the woman said was in a way true. And perhaps it was true also of Dinesh in relation to his own mother, and also to his father and brother, and perhaps to everybody that he'd once known. It didn't matter that he couldn't remember their faces, voices, or characters now, for he carried everything that mattered about them in his body still, they were alive still, not in another world as the

Christian woman had thought, but in the same world, just in a different form, and that at least was something to be grateful for.

All memory must fade eventually of course, even the body's most intimate. It is difficult to imagine forgetting how to walk or forgetting how to speak but enough time confined to a bed and one will eventually forget even how to take a step, enough time spent not speaking to people and one will eventually forget even how to utter a sentence. Such things can usually be relearned it is true, and relearning is never the same as starting from scratch, but even if this meant that what the body has once learned can be never completely be forgotten, that its memory can never be fully erased, all the same such remembrances must eventually dissipate or dwindle, so that even the people one loved most and was closest to will thin with time into ghosts or wraiths, visible briefly every so often in one's movements or gestures, but mostly absent. And so in a way Dinesh was lucky, lucky that it had been so recently that he'd seen his mother, lucky that she was still fresh beneath his skin. In a way he would be lucky even if he were to die soon, for unlike those children in normal places who would live for several decades after the death of their parents his body would not forget the mother with whom he'd spent all his life, by whose hands as a child he had been washed, fed, and clothed, hit on some days and on others caressed, around whom he had grown so used to living that at times he forgot that she was present beside him, feeling as alone with himself when next to her as when he was physically alone, as though they were one and the same person, for what reason after all is there to say that more than one person is present in a room when the hands of one body feed the mouth of the other, when the words spoken by one make the lips of the other part and smile, when all the daily work of each is for the sake of the other, what reason is there to deny that the separate bodies were not different entities but two organs of the same organism? He had been long enough without her to forget what his mother looked and sounded like, had grown used to having no one to look after or to have look after him, but there was no need to be sad he knew for even now she was fresh inside him, even now she was safe and secure within him.

Dinesh pulled the sarong out of the water to see if the soap had been dissolved, but he'd lathered it a little too vigorously apparently, for little yellow flakes of soap were still smeared into the fabric. The water was so soapy he could feel his fingers slipping against each other, and letting it spill out he dropped the bucket down into the well again and let it refill. As he rubbed the two fabrics against each other in the fresh water, twisting and untwisting them to help the soap dissolve, he noticed that his eyes had welled up, that there was moisture in the corner of his eyelashes each time he blinked. How long he'd been urging himself to tears he couldn't tell, but his cheeks were burning lightly from having been tensed, and there was no doubt that if he kept going he would start sooner or later to cry. The drops of salty water secreted by the ducts in his eyes felt like just the smallest part of a vast lake buried somewhere deep inside him, like a massive dam that had sprung a tiny, silent leak, and probably all he had to do in order for it to be released was continue thinking of himself and all that had happened to him in the recent past. He relaxed his hands and let the clothes float in the water, closed his eyes and tried to gather himself. It had been a long time since he'd last cried. It would feel good probably, and might even allow him to remember the past he'd been striving to understand, but all things considered it was best for him to wait till later. He had come to the well only to bathe, and even then only so that

Ganga would see him differently, so that she would admire or even be attracted to him. That was the only reason he'd left her alone in the clearing, and already he'd spent too much time away. If he started crying now it would be difficult to stop, like pissing or shitting or telling a story once you started crying it was not pleasant to stop. In any case he'd feel less vulnerable if he cried in or around the clearing, where he would be able to take his time and not have to worry about being seen or heard. If Ganga was sleeping still he would be able to cry right beside her even, in the soft and solicitous silence of her sleep. He was comfortable enough now being naked beside the well, but crying was an act that involved more vulnerability than bathing or merely being naked, and he was too uneasy to allow himself to cry in such a public space. The area was too open and he needed to be shut off completely in order to cry, as far away from other people and in as enclosed a place as possible. It was possible that the urge would leave him if he waited too long, that even if he tried later on the feeling would not come and he would be unable to cry, but he had no choice he knew, he had to go back to the clearing as soon as he could.

Dinesh squeezed the clothes inside the water tightly one last time, then emptied the water over the concrete. He could rinse them one more time but there was no need, for if there was any soap remaining still it would harden and dry as the clothes dried, and perhaps even provide them with a light scent for a while. Taking up the sarong from the bucket he stretched it out between his hands and twisted it so as to wring out the water. He squeezed it first one way and then the other, watched as the water fell from the fabric first generously and then in stubborn drops. He brought the sarong to his face to breathe in its new lime scent, and feeling the warmth and tiredness of his skin against the cool, freshly cleaned fabric, which till only recently had been as grimy as his body, he felt a vague excitement for the transformation that he too would soon undergo. He unrolled the twisted fabric, spread it out, and hung it out over the well's wall. By the time he had finished extracting all the water from his shirt and underwear and had hung them up too, his hands and feet were soaked, his upper body flecked with drops of water. He stood up and lowered the bucket into the well. He waited for it to fill then pulled it up in quick, rhythmic bursts, and set it on the rim of the wall. There was a small plastic bowl on the platform beside the wall and filling this up in the bucket he bent down slowly towards his feet. He hesitated for a moment, since once he started washing he wouldn't be able to stop halfway he knew, then tipped the water gently over his ankles and shins. He'd wanted to start at his extremities in order to acclimatize himself to the coldness of the water, but the water was actually pleasantly warm, hot almost, a fact he somehow hadn't noticed while washing his clothes. He refilled the bowl and tipped the water over his neck and shoulders, felt its warmth and wetness run softly down the dusty slope of his back. Putting the bowl down he picked up the bucket, raised its full weight up over his neck, and tilting it slightly, careful not to let the splashing make too much noise, let the water empty itself out in a steady, measured stream over his body. It spilled down his chest and stomach and sides, down his groin and slowly past the backs of his legs, wetting his blood-caked, sweat-stained, clay-colored skin. Moving the bucket over his head he let the water fall over his face and greasy hair, down the back of his neck, to the small of his back, the insides of his thighs, let it trickle through his toes and tickle the arches of his feet as it seeped from the concrete into the soil, brown with the blood and dirt of many weeks. Dinesh moved his hands over his thin, wet frame and caressed the contours of his thin chest and torso, as if realizing for the first time that he was in possession of a body. He dropped the bucket once more into the well, raised it heavily up, and poured the water out again slowly over himself, so that all his surfaces were fully wet, so that he was enveloped for the duration of the pouring in a cocoon of warm flowing water.

Dinesh refilled the bucket, put it on the floor, and crouched down beside it. Taking the bowl again with his left hand he began emptying out the water in little parcels over his body, scrubbing meticulously with his right hand at the same time. He began with his feet, scouring the slightly ticklish areas between his toes with his index finger, scraping away with his newly cut nails at the patches just below the bumps of his ankles, where the grime had grafted itself tightly to the skin. He moved up to his calves and knees, rubbing the hairs on his legs so the dirt that encrusted them dissolved away, all the way up to the area between his testicles and the insides of his thighs. Layer after layer of dirt collected into little pleats and fell off his wet skin as he kept scrubbing, layer after layer from his sides, armpits, and neck, from the insides of his elbows and wrists. He rubbed away the sleep that had collected in the inner corners of his eyes and eyelashes and rubbed the fuzz on his chin and jaw that had been stiffened by dry sweat and dirt. With his index finger he pared away at the skin behind his ears, then probing all their ridges he tried to score out the wax that had accumulated inside them. Digging into his belly button he scooped out the material that had developed there, then wetting his backside he picked at all the little pieces of shit that had hardened along the hairs between his buttocks. He drew back his foreskin with his left hand and with his right thumb and forefinger rubbed gently at the head, kneading the cream-colored surface layer so it softened and fell away exposing the pinkness beneath. Refilling the bucket Dinesh poured the warm water out again over his body, slowly, so that all the dirt and grime that he'd loosened but not removed fell away, from his toes, ankles, neck and arms, so that his skin felt newly clean and raw, as if in contact with the air for the first time. He picked up the bar of soap and began to lather himself with it, starting at the feet then moving upwards, taking pleasure in the soap's slipperiness against his skin. He washed away all the lather that had formed over his body, then quickly soaped his hair, once and then again, since his hair was too oily the first time for any lather to form. Drenching his body in the warm water one more time he waved his arms and legs, shook his head violently from side to side in order to throw off all the wetness in his hair, then exhausted crouched back down and leaned back against the well's smooth wet wall.

The area surrounding the well held in a deep silence. A dull silver light fell evenly from the sky, brightening and softening as clouds passed beneath the moon. The outlines of the brush and trees in front of him were sharp and stark, and each blade of grass on the ground seemed razor-edged, as if the world around him were a photograph that had just crystallized under solution. Drops of water trickled down from Dinesh's hair onto his shoulders. They rolled to the ground as his body dried slowly in the cool air, and he shivered imperceptibly as gentle drafts of wind breathed upon his wet skin. Dinesh wrapped his arms around his knees for warmth and hunched his head into his shoulders, gazed at the flaccid penis that drooped down softly between his legs. It was fresh and clean now, free of the smell of toil. All the dirt and dead skin that had coated him, all the rubble and debris of his body had at last been shorn off, leaving him tender and bare, like a warm, living seed. He had returned to himself finally, consisted now of nothing but himself, no dead or extraneous material, only living, breathing substance, porous and naked. It was as though, with the washing away of all the matter that had encrusted his body in the last months, he had freed himself of the hold the recent past had taken of him, as though with the memory inhering in his hair and nails and skin now gone, everything that had happened could be let go of, the present made free finally to take on a different significance, his raw new skin ready, at last, for new memory and for new life.

6

WHEN DINESH ENTERED the safety of the jungle northeast of the camp he began to slow down, then nearing the clearing at last he came at its cusp to a stop, and stood for a moment still in the darkness. In the density of the silence around him he could hear his chest, expanding rapidly and contracting. Lines of perspiration had formed across his upper lip, threaded themselves across his eyebrows, and all over his body sweat was mingling uncomfortably with the moisture still on his freshly washed skin. The walk back from the well had been swift. He hadn't registered it at first but the bath had filled him with a strange vigor, with a desire to use his body as actively and purposefully as possible, so that thinking of Ganga as he made his way past all the people sleeping in the camp, of her chest rising and falling as she lay there on his bed, he found himself moving in quick, urgent strides towards his destination. He was weaker physically than at any other time in his brief adult life it was true, his arms and legs were much thinner than before, his pelvis and ribs visible easily through his skin, but advancing through the camp he had felt strong for some reason, or if not exactly strong then capable at least of strength. He had wanted to sprint all the way back and take hold of Ganga, to cup her entire body in his arms and let her know she could be vulnerable in his presence, that he would take care of her and keep her safe. Once she understood this everything would change he felt, she would open up to him and accept him, would feel no more qualms about being married to him, be eager even to be with him, and this thought impelling him he had moved faster and faster, stopping short of running only to avoid waking anyone in the camp or attracting unnecessary attention, faster and faster as if all he'd been secretly yearning for was waiting there impatiently for him in the clearing.

In the past too, from time to time, Dinesh had felt such a sense of possibility. On some occasions it had been brought about by events that felt important, at the time at least, success on an exam he'd spent time studying for, for example, but most of the time it had been brought on by small, quickly forgotten things, like a glance from a girl he passed by on the street. What exactly caused the feeling was difficult to say, but he could always tell that it was approaching by the sensation of something in his chest expanding, a little at first, then further and further, till it reached the point of bursting, as if his rib cage were holding back something that would soon surge up and sweep across the earth. He would gaze disbelievingly at the razor-edged vividness that everything around him had acquired, as though he'd been lifted up somehow from his environment, sifted out of the small section of the world in which he'd been absorbed, as though he'd been made aware, for a brief moment, of a world vaster than and more independent of him, a world that he had the chance, in some way, to encompass in its entirety. How this encompassing could actually be accomplished he never had any concrete idea, needless to say, nothing he could actually do at such times ever seemed adequate to what he felt, no action he was capable of ever fully articulated or sustained it. He would have run unstopping across the earth's circumference if he were able, fast enough to gather up the whole world in his arms, he would have dug down through the soil all the way to the core of the earth, if he could, but his body obviously was too heavy and burdensome, his arms and legs incapable of the necessary movements. No matter how hard he tried to find an activity by which to fully express himself at such times he would always remain at a loss, and as a result the sense of possibility that swept over him would slowly begin to recede, till he returned with sad inevitability to the small and habitual world of which he was ordinarily a part, only a diminishing glimmer remaining of the possibilities he had briefly felt.

Dinesh touched the smooth trunk of the tree closest to him with his hand, leaned forward so he could feel its cool bark against his cheek. He'd had on this occasion some idea of what he could do, he needed to find Ganga, he knew, to embrace her, and to show her how he felt so that she would finally accept him, but standing now at the cusp of the clearing, his clothes no longer dripping but damp still from having been washed, hanging down heavily from his shoulders and waist, clinging to his back and legs, he began to feel that his plan was unrealistic, that maybe it wouldn't be possible at all. He could sense Ganga's still somewhat unfamiliar presence behind the ferns, permeating the more recognizable presences of the rock, the earthen bed, and the border of pebbles and stones. How would they interact, having been absent from each other for so long? Would they be able to resume their marriage at the point they'd left off, or would they have to begin once more from scratch? Ganga was asleep still probably, but most likely when she woke she wouldn't be in the mood to listen to what he wanted to say, most likely she would again be too upset or distant to talk. Most likely she would be annoyed at his presence and his attempts to communicate, as she had been when they came to the clearing after the marriage, and if she wasn't annoyed then probably she'd be uninterested in paying attention to him anyway, regardless of whether or not he'd bathed. Even if they did retain the small degree of understanding they'd acquired in the few hours they had spent together awake, how would he be able to share with her what he wanted to in any case, given the situation they were in? It was as though all this while he'd forgotten that Ganga's mother and brother had died only two weeks before, that her father had only just abandoned her. Even if now unlike earlier she were willing to talk how would she be in a state to understand the feelings he wanted to express, and what in any case would he say to begin with?

A light breeze blew past the top of the canopy, and the leaves around the clearing shook gently before falling still. Dinesh let go of the branch he was holding, which inadvertently he'd begun to clench, and breathing in he stretched out his arms in an effort to loosen up his body. Perhaps his anxiety didn't really have to do with the context in which Ganga and he had married. Perhaps it was actually a natural, normal feeling, something that would have affected him even if they had met in the course of ordinary life. Perhaps it had nothing to do with the fact that the two of them had been separated from their families and homes, or alienated from everything that was once their own, or brought together without any real reason while all around them the shells were falling generously, body parts being scattered here and there like twigs and stones in the dirt. Perhaps his anxiety was not so different from how he used to feel long ago when he was still studying, when for whatever reason he had an opportunity to talk to one of the pretty students from the girls' school nearby, perhaps what he was feeling was only the natural, normal nervousness of a boy, about to meet a girl.

Dinesh took in another long breath and walked a few steps into the clearing. Careful to avoid stepping on the larger plants, he stood up on his toes, and tried to make out the bed over the ferns that obscured it. Lying there quietly, bathed in the blue light that fell in through the break in the canopy, was Ganga. She was occupying only a narrow section of the bed, her cheek pressed upon the sari that she'd laid out earlier over the tarpaulin sheet, her left arm flung behind her head. She was if anything in a deeper state of sleep than when he'd left, and most probably she hadn't noticed that he'd been gone. There was still a chance she could wake up as he approached though, and it would be best if he found a way to explain where he was coming from. He could say he'd needed to urinate and that he hadn't been gone very long, though then she might notice that his clothes were damp, that they were a lot cleaner than before, and also that he now smelled of lime. Maybe he could just admit to having washed his body, but say it was at a pump well close by instead of all the way back at the clinic. There remained also the issue of whether to admit to having used the soap and the pair of scissors, or whether to put them back discreetly in the bag and pretend he'd never taken out anything at all, but not wanting to be burdened by these problems when Ganga was finally just a few feet in front of him Dinesh drew in another breath, took four long, loping steps over the vegetation, and came to a stop before the pillowed end of the bed. Ganga stirred slightly, and brought her outstretched arm back down beneath her shoulder. Eyes still closed she furrowed her eyebrows as though in surprise or objection, then blinking several times, she slowly began to open her eyes. She looked first at Dinesh's feet, which were directly in line with her head, then up at his thighs, and then at his face. She gazed at him for some time, a look of slight confusion in her face, as though unable to recognize him. Dinesh became afraid she wouldn't remember that they'd gotten married at all, but then sitting up a little Ganga looked at the sari she was lying on, at the bag and pots and pans lying just beyond her feet, and the trees all around them, and her features came together in slow recognition. She looked back up at Dinesh.

Where are you going?

She said this somewhat loudly, as though despite knowing where she was, she wasn't yet aware of the time.

Nowhere, whispered Dinesh, lowering his voice to convey that they shouldn't talk too loudly. I had to go to the bathroom.

He took off his slippers and crouched down at the foot of the bed. Ganga withdrew her feet, either to keep some distance from him or to give him more space. She shuffled back across the bed so as to recline against the rock, and began rubbing the sleep from her eyes.

Sorry for waking you up. I was trying to be quiet.

Ganga continued massaging her eyes in a slow, circular motion. She nodded vaguely to indicate that an apology wasn't needed, then began kneading her forehead and cheeks with her thumbs.

Were you sleeping well? You must have been tired, you fell asleep as soon as we got back from the camp.

Ganga straightened her legs out across the bed and shrugged her shoulders.

I suppose so.

She stretched her arms out and let out a little yawn, then clasped her hands together neatly over her lap and looked up into the darkness of the jungle ahead of her. Dinesh studied her from his slightly awkward crouching position by the foot of the bed. Her long back was gracefully arched, despite the fact she'd just woken, and her eyes were fully open. Her gaze was focused on a single point among the trees, as if she were dwelling on some fact or trying to remember some detail. It couldn't have been later than midnight or one o'clock, but it didn't seem like she was planning to go back to sleep. She couldn't have been asleep for more than three or four hours altogether, and it would have made sense if she needed more time to sleep, but maybe three or four hours was enough for her, for the edge at least to be taken off her fatigue, maybe now that she was awake she wanted to stay up and talk to him.

Are you thirsty?

Ganga looked at Dinesh, slightly surprised, then nodded. Dinesh turned around towards the beige bag, got on his knees, and leaning forward over it zipped open the main compartment. Pretending to search for the plastic water bottle he'd seen during his perusal earlier that night, he took out the soap and scissors as discreetly as he could from his shirt pocket, not just the soap and scissors but also the small package containing his hair and nails, and unzipping the bag's side pocket deposited them inside stealthily. He then pulled the bottle out of the main compartment, turned back around to Ganga and handed it to her casually. She hesitated a moment before extending her hand to receive it, and Dinesh realized the mistake he'd made. In a way it was true of course, now that they were married, that he was entitled to open her bag by himself, but opening it in front of Ganga without asking for permission nevertheless felt like an act of violence, like a refusal to acknowledge the primacy of her relationship to it. Dinesh wondered what he could say to excuse or explain himself but before he could do so Ganga leaned forward wordlessly and took the bottle from him. She unscrewed its lid with her long graceful fingers, raised the bottle up, and tipping it so that the opening was over her mouth but not in contact with her lips she let the water trickle delicately onto her teeth and tongue, down softly into her throat. She lowered the bottle, raised it up and took another sip, then screwed the lid back firmly over the top. She placed the bottle on the ground to her right, glanced at Dinesh again, then looked down at her lap.

Instead of returning to his former position Dinesh shuffled back towards the rock and sat back against it, two or three feet to the left of where Ganga sat. It was hard to be certain, but she didn't seem so much hurt or angered at what he had done, as surprised or slightly disconcerted, as though by means of his action she'd come to a more concrete appreciation of her situation than she'd possessed in the first few minutes of waking. There was a faint hint of sadness in her eyes, but it was not necessarily different from what he'd noticed before the marriage, when he'd seen her working by herself in the clinic or combing her hair outside her father's tent, a sadness that probably had less to do with his opening her bag or their now being married, Dinesh felt, than with disappointment about how the world was in general.

He looked at her and spoke quietly.

Do you want to go back to sleep?

Ganga looked at him. She shook her head, and looked back down at her hands. Once I get up I can't go back to sleep. I don't sleep that long anyway, only a few hours usually.

Dinesh hesitated for a moment, then spoke again.

Do you sleep during the day?

She shook her head.

Don't you get tired?

She shrugged, still looking down. It depends. Usually by evening I'm exhausted from working in the clinic, so it isn't hard to fall asleep.

Otherwise I don't really get tired. I didn't do any work in the clinic today, but I was tired because the night before I didn't sleep at all.

There was a brief silence, but before Dinesh could ask her to elaborate she looked up quickly from her lap and spoke. Did you sleep?

Yesterday night or just now?

Just now.

He shook his head. No.

I can move if you want to sleep for a while, she said bending forward as if to get up.

No, it's okay. It's difficult for me to fall sleep.

Dinesh tried to think of something else to add, slightly embarrassed for making this admission, then patted the rock behind him casually, as if to indicate its solidity. I was resting against the rock while you were sleeping, so I'm not tired anyway.

I don't mind moving.

It's okay. Don't worry.

Ganga let herself fall back against the rock, and pretending to look straight ahead Dinesh did his best to study her again through the corner of his eye. Her ponytail had slackened a little while she'd slept. Several strands of hair were hanging carelessly over the side of her face, no longer as tightly plastered to her head as before, and her face too seemed limber and more elastic than before, especially in the moments in which she spoke. Her sentences were still short and she still spoke slowly, with a kind of indifference, but the inertness that had been in her voice earlier in the day was no longer present, and she no longer sounded remote. Everything she said now seemed more connected somehow to the expression on her face, as though despite being sad she was able now at least to understand the words that were coming out of her mouth.

Ganga slapped the back of her neck. She scratched the area vigorously for a while then leaned forward and began to scratch her ankles.

Did mosquitoes bite while you were asleep?

She nodded without stopping to look up.

That's the only problem with this place, the whole jungle is full of mosquitoes. In the camp at least there are no mosquitoes.

There are mosquitoes in the camp too. The only difference is that there are so many people in the camp that the mosquitoes never have to focus on a single person.

Unsure what to say Dinesh shifted his back a little against the rock, and dwelled for a moment on the softness of the dry moss and lichen on his lower back.

I remember seeing a neem tree near the edge of the camp. I can collect some of the nuts to burn, that will keep them away.

Ganga tucked her hands in neatly under her thighs and leaned forward again from the rock, too preoccupied with some thought apparently to respond to what he'd said. She gazed for a long time at the trees in front of them, as though she could distinguish something in the darkness, then turned again to Dinesh.

Where do you go during the shelling? Do you stay here?

No. He shook his head and motioned east. There's an upside-down boat about five minutes from here, some fisherman must have dragged it into the jungle instead of leaving it by the shore. Usually I crawl inside that. It's quite big, both of us can definitely fit inside.

Is it strong enough to guard against shrapnel?

Yes, the wood is very thick. Shrapnel is less of a problem in the jungle anyway, because of all the trees. But if you want we can dig a trench beneath it tomorrow, just in case.

We can think about it tomorrow.

Maybe it would be for the best. I can do it by myself in the morning, it won't be difficult.

Ganga nodded her head in acquiescence, as if the suggestion were acceptable to her or even pleasing. She drew back a few strands of hair that had fallen over her face and then tucked her hands back under her thighs. There was a looseness in the way she moved her body that made her seem more comfortable than earlier in the day, more relaxed, less on guard. Dinesh too felt more at ease, no longer worried about whether they had to resume their marriage from scratch. It was as though, in the brief period of time in which they had been separated from each other, they had actually grown closer to each other, more understanding or aware of each other. Maybe some deep inner affinity between them was being uncovered, maybe their new comfort was a sign of some more ancient understanding that had always existed between them, though probably not, Dinesh knew, for however pleasing those possibilities might have been to consider, the actual explanation was probably more mundane. Even in normal life after all the second meeting with a new person was always much easier than the first, the third easier than the second, and so on, even if nothing concrete changed between meetings. It was in the time between meetings that each body came to terms with all the newness and strangeness of the other after all, to its smell and presence and speech and manner, it was in the periods of separation that the muscles and nerves of each person were molded and tuned in response to the other, so that when the two bodies met again there was, suddenly, much less awkwardness or difficulty. When it came to getting to know a person the periods of time spent apart were just as important as the periods spent together, and probably that was why things were easier now between them, not because they were in some way meant or destined for one another.

There was silence except for the soft back and forth of their breathing, Ganga's light and regular, Dinesh's heavier and a little faster. The rhythms of their rising and falling chests accompanied each other softly in parallel, intersecting occasionally when they fell out of phase, then gradually drawing back together. Dinesh wiped away the tiny drops of sweat that had formed across his forehead and drew his hand back across his hair, still cool and wet from bathing. Even if they'd only gotten more used to each other, even if their new ease around each other was unremarkable, even predictable, still he couldn't help feeling hopeful that it could be a conduit through which something further and more intimate might pass between them.

Dinesh shifted his body a little closer to Ganga and tilted towards her, so that they were separated by no more than a foot.

Do you work in the clinic every day?

Ganga glanced at him and looked back down.

On most days. Whenever I can.

I've seen you there once or twice. I've gone to help a few times too, but only immediately after the shelling, to help move the wounded. I can't imagine working in the clinic every single day. It must be difficult, no, with all the blood and everything? You must be a selfless person.

Ganga pulled her hands out from under her thighs and clasped them once more neatly over her lap. I only go there for my own sake, she said without looking up. It's good to have something to do, whatever it is, it's better than having to wait.

You go there to be distracted?

Ganga opened her mouth to say something, then stopped. Dinesh waited for her to speak but in the silence that followed all she did was tilt her head to the side and continue looking at her hands, not as though she hadn't heard what he said, but as though his question hadn't really been a question, or as though her silence was itself an answer. Her lips stayed parted for a while then closed, and leaning to her right she picked up one of the pebbles from the border of the bed and began rolling it about soundlessly on her palm.

Dinesh felt an urge to say something, but hesitated. He wanted to respond to Ganga's silence by accepting it somehow, by acknowledging what it contained, but at the same time the thought of disrupting it by speaking seemed in some way inappropriate. There had been silence between them before, of course, as they had stood transfixed after the marriage ceremony, as they had sat next to each other for the first time in the clearing, and as they had eaten together afterwards in the camp, but this silence felt different somehow. The earlier silence had been the silence that existed between people living in different worlds. It had been the silence that existed between everybody in the camp, the silence between two people separated by a sheer wall of polished stone. The silence that was present between them now on the other hand was one that connected them rather than separated them. It charged the air between them so completely that the slightest movement by either one of them could be sensed at once by the other, so that their bodies were as if suspended together in a medium that was outside time.

The sky above them brightened as a heavy mass of cloud passed out from under the moon, illuminating everything that till then had been concealed by the darkness. The blue-and-purple fabric of the sari glowed dully beneath them, and in front of them the dark greens of the ferns and the grays and browns of the trees became faintly visible.

That's why I go to the clinic too, said Dinesh softly. Even if you don't talk to anybody, it's good once in a while to see other people and to move.

Ganga's expression remained unchanged but she stopped rolling the pebble, so that it lay still in the center of her palm. She stared calmly at it for a while, then put it back in its place on the bed's decorative border. Looking at Dinesh she motioned to the border.

Was this here already?

What do you mean?

Were all these stones arranged like this before you came here?

He shook his head. I put them there myself, to make a border. I got the idea when I was picking up all the rocks and stones stuck in the soil.

Ganga pointed to the mound of earth at the head of the bed. Did you make that too?

He nodded. I carved it out of the soil, to use as a pillow.

It's funny that you took so much care to make a sleeping space when you can't fall asleep.

Dinesh looked at Ganga for a moment, then looked up at the trees at the edge of the clearing. The sky darkened as clouds passed once more beneath the moon and the trees and everything else around them returned to their indistinguishable shades of black and dark blue.

There was silence once more except for their breathing, which seemed to have come a little closer together, hers just a little faster, a little heavier than before, his just a little slower, a little gentler. The faint buzz of a mosquito trembled above their heads, then faded into the darkness.

Why can't you fall asleep?

Dinesh glanced at Ganga, who was looking at him inquisitively, then returned his gaze quickly to the trees.

I don't know. I'll lie down, and close my eyes, but for some reason I can't sleep.

You can't fall asleep at all?

Dinesh could feel Ganga's eyes upon him, searching him, but he did his best to fix his gaze on the darkness ahead. It wasn't that he feared that by looking into his eyes Ganga would come to realize how much the recent months had affected him, for most likely she could already tell from the fact that he couldn't sleep and from the expression of shame now on his face. He could endure to some degree her thinking of him as fragile or as incapacitated, it wasn't pleasant but he had no choice, but what he couldn't bear was having to look her in the eyes while she was dwelling on such thoughts simultaneously, in the same way, perhaps, that if someone opens the door without warning while one is changing one's clothes one finds it impossible, in that moment, despite being confronted by their immediate presence, to look the person in the eye. Making eye contact at such times gave you no choice but to see yourself through the eyes of the person looking at you, to acknowledge things you were ashamed of that till then you'd managed to hide from yourself or ignore, and in such situations therefore it was imperative, even before attempting to cover up one's nudity, to avert one's eyes. Dinesh lowered his head, and tried to stare down into his lap.

No, he said quietly in response.

The sky above them brightened soundlessly then once more grew dark. In the silence that surrounded them another high, trembling buzz glanced past their heads. Dinesh felt a light pricking near the back of his neck, but he remained motionless, not wanting to disturb the air by raising even a hand. In the strangely magnified pinch of the mosquito's bite he could sense, vividly, the stillness of Ganga's body beside him, as though she too felt compelled not to move. Bending down beside her only an hour or two earlier so that his face was just inches from her skin, he had been hesitant, despite wanting to come to some kind of understanding of who she was, to touch Ganga for even a second, out of fear she would turn out to be unreal, to be fake or in some way illusory. Sitting beside her now however it was as though he could be sure, for the first time since they'd met, that reaching out and touching her, he would really be able to feel the warmth of her skin.

The pricking on his neck reached a peak, and weightlessly the mosquito took flight. The sharpness of the bite began to dissipate, but Dinesh remained where he was, completely unmoving against the rock.

In the past too he had felt this strange desire for stillness, not often, but more than once or twice. He would be sitting with one or two of his friends on the outskirts of the village at late evening, cross-legged on the earth, the darkening blue sky spread out before them in the distance. What they spoke about at such times he could no longer say, but there were moments, Dinesh could remember, when their conversation would begin to slow down, when everything they said would seem to circle around some strangely intangible object, around a place or thing they could sense in the vicinity even if it couldn't be seen. All their questions, answers, pauses, and responses, all their additions, hesitations, and elaborations, each and every utterance they made at such times felt like a delicate attempt to move closer to this object, so that tentatively, intuitively, stopping and starting, their conversation would seem to spiral around this sensed but unseen place or thing, drawing closer and closer to it, moving more carefully and more nervously as smaller and smaller circles were drawn round it, till finally, with much apprehension, each of them fully absorbed in what was going on, something was said that could not possibly get nearer to what they sought. When such a point was reached they were able to sense it almost instinctively, even if they couldn't see or touch what they had found, as though what they had been searching for all along was not so much a place or a thing as a mood, a mood which had been obscurely understood from the very beginning as a means by which they could come together, by which they might move out of their own separate worlds, onto a plane in which they could recognize and understand each other fully for a brief time. Having put them at last in the presence of this mood such conversations always, if they succeeded, had to end, had to come to a point where nothing more could be said, where not even a movement could be made, for just as a butterfly perched on the edge of a blade of grass, so lightly that the blade quivers slightly but does not bend, can be approached only up to a certain distance before it folds back its weightless wings nervously and twitches, after which the very slightest noise, a heavy breath or the cracking of a joint, will prompt it to silently flit away, so also they were aware that the mood that had been so patiently and yearningly and painstakingly sought could be caused, by the most innocuous further word or motion, to slip away, leaving them stranded once more in their own separate worlds, leaving each one of them once more alone.

The mood that held them together never lasted very long of course, it either dissipated gradually, or was punctured or pierced by some outside interruption, and sooner or later the same would happen to him and Ganga too, Dinesh knew, unless they could find another way of sustaining it, a way that allowed themselves and the air between them to move. The slightest wrong sound or movement could destroy the delicate balance they'd already achieved, could take them away from the world they had found, but all the same it was better to risk the chance of destroying it outright in an effort to prolong its existence, Dinesh felt, than to let it slip away on its own. His breath still held back he inched just a little closer to Ganga, so that their shoulders lightly touched. He straightened out his folded knees so their legs were lying parallel, in contact almost at the calves. Against his stiffly erect back he could feel the new section of rock, beneath his tightly locked knees the airy fabric of the cool new section of sari. He became, once more, rooted to the spot. Beside him he could sense Ganga's rigidity, her body also completely still, more so if possible than before, her chest also neither rising nor falling, as if she too understood the purpose of what he had done. How she felt it was hard to say for on the one hand she did nothing to acknowledge his movement, but on the other hand she did nothing to object. He didn't want to get too close to her if she didn't want him to, he didn't want to make her do anything she didn't want to do, and he could still pull back if he wanted, since he hadn't actually touched her, after all, and had done nothing to commit himself to touching her at all. There was the possibility that she did want him to touch her though, that perhaps she'd come to like him over the course of the day, found him easier to be close to now that he'd bathed, perhaps even attractive too, and the longer she remained there right next to him without moving the more possible this seemed, for she had after all seemed engaged while they'd spoken, she'd asked him questions of her own initiative, as though she really did want to talk to him, and so perhaps the reason she remained as completely still as him now was simply that she was paralyzed by nervousness too, that she too simply didn't know what to do.

Ganga's hands were lying half-open beside each other on her lap, cupping each other loosely with fingers intertwined, and seeing them through the corner of his eye Dinesh reached out instinctively with his right hand towards her lap. He took the thumb of her left hand between his index finger and thumb and clasped it firmly yet delicately, in the same way one might hold a fresh sheet of paper by its corner so as not to smudge it with dirty hands. The tip of her thumb, so small and perfect, remained limp between his fingers. It felt strange to have a thing so autonomously alive in his touch, to have a thing so precious completely still in his hand. As gently as he could, he caressed it. He moved his fingertips over her hard smooth nail, across the intricately etched skin that formed her thumbprint, tried to listen to the quiet beating of blood through the tiny, finely articulated vessels underneath. Opening out his other fingers he brought them around the rest of her hand, so that the whole of her hand was immersed in his, and then suddenly, like a tautly stretched piece of elastic that has just been cut, his body slackened. Without warning, as if the mood established by their conversation no longer had to be sustained by stillness, as if like scaffolding that is removed when the roof between two walls has been set in place, the air around them could finally be disturbed, Dinesh felt his chest, which had been held back for how long he didn't know, suddenly falling, the air inside his lungs suddenly receding. Beside him Ganga's chest also fell, then rose, and fell, exactly in time with his, as if having simultaneously stopped breathing just a moment before, they could breathe in unison now as long as they remained in contact.

Dinesh looked at Ganga. Her head was lowered and he couldn't tell whether her eyes were open or closed, but her eyebrows were relaxed, like buoys floating soundlessly on a deep, calm sea. Not taking his eyes off her face he squeezed her hand a little, to make sure it remained real even after the slackening of their muscles, then immediately eased his hold again, as though the slightest pressure could harm her. It was strange to think that the hand he was holding belonged to the face he was looking at. It felt so strange inside his own hand, soft and warm and small, simultaneously alive and still, so different from the hand of the little boy he'd seen that morning. Dinesh traced a line across it silently with his finger, from her thumb lightly along the vein that stretched past the inside of Ganga's wrist. He followed the quiet pulse along her long, slender arm, up over the scar that interrupted skin otherwise smooth as a newly bought bar of soap, till his fingertip descended into the hollow of her elbow, where it paused, and remained still. Ganga's eyes remained closed, but soundlessly her lips parted. Dinesh took hold of both her hands with his left hand, brought his right arm over her head and around her back, and clasped her far shoulder gently. He hesitated for a moment, then drawing her closer to him and simultaneously moving closer to her he held their bodies together so their thighs pressed against each other and also their calves. Ganga remained slack at first, unresponsive, but then inclined her head towards him so that it rested on his shoulder, the crown of her head against his ear and cheek, pushing into the side of his head with her own as though trying to burrow into him. Dinesh brought his right arm down from her shoulder to her lower back, the line of her spine upon his palm, then leaning forward brought his left arm across to her far shoulder so that he was encompassing her body with both his arms. He slid his right hand from her lower back around her waist, which was slender enough almost for him to cup with that one hand alone, and pulled their bodies tighter together so that even the sensitive mounds of their knees were rubbing one another firmly. They moved closer and closer, held each other tighter and tighter, and then suddenly Ganga's body seemed to fold forward and tilt downwards and instinctively Dinesh's body followed it too, his arms loosening their hold but not letting go, so that they both fell together sideways onto the bed facing each other, their heads overshooting the earthen pillow by just a little, their bodies exposed to each other full on for the first time, chests touching but only very faintly and their waists also and their feet. Dinesh's arms were still around her body and he wanted to draw her in more tightly so he could feel her breasts push against him through her frock but their heads were facing each other almost, were far enough apart for eye contact to be made, and though they'd both taken care that their gazes didn't meet, he looking only into her neck and she only into his shoulder, the possibility alone was enough to make him hesitate.

They were married now. In a way it was only natural for them to have desire, to want to satisfy themselves for the first time, though whether or not Ganga really felt this way Dinesh wanted to be completely sure. She was pressing her head against him as though in order to be closer to him, her lips were parted and her eyebrows relaxed as if she wanted to fall into him, but perhaps she simply felt obliged to be this way because he was her husband now and she his wife. It was hard to imagine that she was acting of course, she seemed too forthright to hide her feelings in that way, but at the same time it was equally hard, if not harder, to imagine that she was actually attracted to him. Dinesh raised his right hand, hesitantly, and placed his index and middle finger lightly on the hem of her sleeve. He traced her upper arm delicately down from the shoulder to the elbow, moving from her arm and descending into the curve of her waist before rising once more with her hip. Ganga's body stiffened and slackened. She inched closer to him, so her toes were on his shins, the tops of her thighs on his, the softness of her breasts grazing his chest. In a way he wouldn't even have been upset if she didn't want to make love immediately, in a way he would have even been relieved, for though in a sense he wanted to and though it was something he knew he should experience before he died, it was hard to know whether he himself was actually capable, even if after so many years of waiting he now actually had the chance. It wasn't that he didn't think she was beautiful, or that he didn't feel any physical desire for her, for each time she inhaled and her waist was drawn in he felt an undeniable urge to tighten his arms around her and get closer, but at the same time it was not exactly a sexual urge, this desire to press closer, or not at least fully sexual, since even with her breath hot on his neck, her breasts breathing heavily upon his chest, and her groin pressed up against his, their bodies separated by only two thin layers of fabric, he was unable to feel between his legs any hardness. It had been a long time since he'd last felt any hardness it was true, but he could remember clearly how in the past he would often feel himself hardening without warning against the fabric of his shorts or trousers or sarong, how he would grow not just heavier but harder and stiffer till it began almost to hurt, till the rest of his body was limp in comparison, and he could tell now without difficulty that despite the heaviness that had grown between his legs there was still, for some reason, no hardness.

Ganga had brought both her arms around him so they were both clutching each other, she squeezing tightly and he also, their bodies pressed together so that there was hardly any room for thrusting or resisting. Closing his eyes and trying to focus, Dinesh did his best to dwell on the undulation of her body against his, on the rising of her chest and the sinking of her waist. He tried to think of her slender back and sharp collarbones, and of the fact that she wanted to make love with him, with him rather than anybody else, after having known him for only a day. He tried to think of the fact that she was alive, that there was blood pulsing in the veins beneath her skin, that an entire world of thought and feeling subsisted autonomously inside of her, which he wanted to help look after, to take care of and keep safe in every pos-

sible way, and wrapping his arms more tightly around Ganga he tried
to somehow convey this to her, to let her know that he was strong
enough, that he could do anything for her that she needed and that
she could be happy together with him. That was all he wanted her to
know, if she felt that and believed it then everything would be all right
he knew, everything would be okay, the heavy softness between his
legs would harden, and they would be able to make love like a married couple on their first night. Lifting his head up slightly from her
neck Dinesh placed his temple alongside Ganga's and tried to listen,
as if by juxtaposing their individual pulses and measuring the differ-
ences in rhythm he could find out whether her thoughts were the same
as his, whether or not she too believed he was capable of taking care
of her and whether she even wanted that, furrowing his eyebrows as
one of her legs insinuated itself between his, screwing shut his eyes as
she caressed the side of his face with hers, doing his best to concentrate but all the same unable as he pressed his temple to hers to obtain
any sign, unable to glean anything but the hardness of her head, the
sheer fact of her skull, unyielding as a wall, so that stiffening his body
and tightening his arms around her he brought his lips up to her ear at
last and spoke, his voice quiet and a little shaky.

Are you happy we're married?

Ganga stopped moving.

Perhaps she hadn't heard him. Gently, he repeated the question.

He waited for her to respond but she remained silent.

Are you happy that we're married?

Ganga drew her head back a little.

What do you mean?

Are you happy that we're together here?

Their bodies were still pressed together but were now completely rigid. The warmth and moisture of Ganga's skin emanated up, and seemed to hold everything still.

What is there to be happy or sad about?

Dinesh's arms loosened very slightly around her back.

Things just happen and we have to accept them. Happiness and sadness are for people who can control what happens to them.

Dinesh's arms and legs slackened. Ganga remained as she was for a moment, then retracted her leg slowly from in between his, so that his legs came together once more. Between his calves he could feel a heavy film of perspiration, and underneath his body the moist folds of the sari, ruffled now by all their movement. His chest was sinking of its own accord, as though he were losing his breath, and the slight heaviness his penis had acquired was dissipating. He tried thinking again of Ganga's body, of the small of her back and her sinking waist, but his penis continued getting smaller, withdrawing more and more into his legs. He strained the muscle deep inside his groin, the muscle that when strained caused it to jerk up a little, that when strained in the right conditions could lead, he knew from when he was younger, to an erection, he strained this muscle, a second time and then a third, but no desire returned, only regret. Ganga's breathing had become calmer, and her arms were draped only loosely now over his body. All Dinesh could feel of himself, no matter how he tried, was an imperceptible quivering between his legs. He strained one more time and felt even less, then one more time and felt nothing at all. His body completely limp, as if it had completely let go, he buried his head as deep as he could inside the seclusion of Ganga's neck, inside the small, private hollow between her collarbone and the side of her neck, and began, without any warning, to cry.

7

IT WAS ONLY WHEN his crying had softened to a whimpering and then to a silent quivering that Dinesh began to discern the sound, rising and falling, like a muted or muffled calling, that was coming not far from where they lay. It came as a surprise not so much because the jungle around the clearing was always silent at that time of night, as it usually was in the daytime too, but because it brought to his awareness the more general fact that all the while an entire world had continued to exist outside him. His face was still buried in Ganga's neck, and they were still lying on the sari draped over the bed. His arms were hanging loosely around her body, hers around his, the soft gusts of wind that came in through the trees around them still breathing coolly upon his skin, but for the duration of his crying it had felt as if he were the only thing there, as if there was nothing in the world but his thin body and small, fragile penis, which earlier in his life would lengthen and harden independently of him, occupy at times more space than had been apportioned to it, but which now had withdrawn so much it could no longer be felt between his legs, like an amputated limb that only seemed to still exist. It was funny, in a way, after all he'd seen and done, that it was this fact that had at last caused him to cry. He couldn't remember having cried even when his mother had died, he was closer to her to than to anybody else and still he probably hadn't even shed a tear, but so many months later the mere fact of his penis being unable to rise was enough to make the ducts of his eyes fill up and his Adam's apple recede into his throat. He had known that he shouldn't give in to the urge overwhelming him, that he should restrain himself at least while he was in front of Ganga, but before he could help it tears were streaming down his cheeks and it became clear that he would be unable to stop, which comforted him in a way, because really he wanted to let everything spill out, to let himself go completely in fact, so that continuing to think of his penis dangling uselessly from his dilapidated body, imagining himself rolling it up tenderly in a square piece of sari fabric and burying it in the earth, he had begun to cry harder and harder, with more and more of his body, so that his chest began to spasm, so that every part of him was shaking, till he became at last wholly lost in the act of crying.

When he was eight or maybe nine years old his mother had hit him once for something, what exactly for he couldn't remember, only that the beating had been unfair and that he hadn't deserved it. Running from the kitchen in tears into the bedroom he shared with his brother and grandmother he had closed the door so that he could be alone, then slipped into the lightless space under the wooden bed on which their grandmother slept. There was only about a half foot between the floor and the frame, but he was thin and managed to insinuate himself all the way inside on his hands and feet, the dry smell of dust thick in his nostrils, his head pressed against the planks that supported the mattress above him. He swiveled around slowly so that his feet were upon the base of the wall, and lowering his forehead down to the cool hard floor as if to pray he began to cry, urging himself to tears over the fact that he had been wrongfully hurt, dwelling not only on what had just happened but also, one by one, on all the times he could remember his mother having hurt him in the past, knowingly though perhaps not consciously using each instance to goad himself on. Why exactly he had wanted to lose himself in this condition wasn't so hard to understand, crying for yourself was gratifying after all, it was a way of taking care of yourself, even if it involved some pain, though why he had needed to hide himself in order to do so, why he was unable to do so in the open, was a little more difficult to say. Perhaps it had to do with the fact that in crying for yourself you were acknowledging your vulnerability, acknowledging that despite your various efforts and postures you can be and have been hurt by the world. In crying for yourself the gritted jaw or deadened gaze or feigned indifference by which at other times you managed to protect yourself from everything that happened to you had to be given up, and perhaps in order to bear the period of raw contact with the world that followed this letting go you needed to be in a safe place, a place where you could not be harmed. Unless perhaps he'd needed to hide not in order to protect himself, but because rather the indignation he'd felt was at odds with the injustice, because in the face of all the other injustices of the world what his mother had done to him was a trifle, and gave him no real justification to cry for himself. Perhaps this was why as one grew older one broke down and cried for oneself less, because tears for oneself could only come when one ignored the suffering of everybody else, or pretended at least that it was not significant. As you got older the suffering of others became more difficult to ignore, as you saw more of life and became more a part of the world it became harder to imagine that the pain you faced was unique and in need of special attention, and as a result crying for yourself felt indulgent unless you could pretend that nobody else existed, or that your own pain was different and more exceptional, and to do this perhaps it was easier if you found somewhere to be completely alone.

Why exactly he had wanted to bury his face so deep in Ganga's neck was difficult to say but in any case, after having been so long lost in the intoxicating ache of his convulsing body, in the water of his endlessly emptying eyes, a soft, inviting exhaustion had begun to wash over him, and hearing for the first time the muffled voice rising and falling in the distance, Dinesh had remembered suddenly that lying at his side was a girl he had just gotten married to, a person who'd suffered far more than he in the recent past, that they were lying in a clearing in the jungle, just northeast of a camp that contained tens of thousands of evacuees, that there was, in short, a world that existed beyond him. Their bodies were still pressed lightly together, and Ganga's arm was still loosely draped over him, as if she hadn't known how exactly to respond to what happened, whether to comfort and console him or whether to remove herself and let him cry on his own. Ashamed suddenly for having been preoccupied with himself for so long, for having sought safety in Ganga's neck when it was he who should have been consoling her, Dinesh stiffened his muscles and tried to suppress the shivers still running through his body. He raised his head up a little from Ganga's completely drenched neck, so that their faces and necks were no longer touching but in such a way that they would still be unable to see each other, and unsure whether he'd actually heard anything or whether it was just his imagination, he closed his eyes and tried to listen. The call rose up once more; it lingered in the canopy, and then fell away. Ganga's body moved a little beside him, as though she'd heard it too, but Dinesh tried to remain still. He wanted to look at Ganga to verify that she had also heard the sound, which was coming from a section of jungle not far from the clearing, it seemed, probably fifteen or twenty meters to the north or northwest, but looking at her would also mean acknowledging the fact that he'd been crying, which was not something he felt capable yet of doing.

The sound rose up, continued for a little longer this time, and fell away. Ganga shifted once more, decisively this time, as if she wanted to move, and having no choice but to respond Dinesh wiped his eyes and cheeks on the sleeve of his shirt and shifted onto his elbows, careful to keep his eyes averted. Ganga withdrew her arm from him and bending her legs sat forward and rested her head on her knees. Dinesh wondered for a moment whether he should say something to apologize, whether he should make some attempt to explain why he had cried so much, but what he could have said he didn't know, and in any case there was no indication on Ganga's face that anything had happened. It was as though she wanted to pretend she had not been there or that it had not occurred, and as if she could sense without having to look at him that he was wondering whether or not to bring up the subject, she turned towards him and spoke preemptively.

What was that sound?

Dinesh shook his head, looking at Ganga then quickly looking away. I'm not sure.

It rose up again—whether it was calling or speaking or crying it was impossible to tell—then enduring as long as it could, fell away. There was silence for twenty or thirty seconds, as if the voice wanted to rest and gather strength, and then it rose up freshly once more.

Have you heard it before?

No. Never.

It probably wasn't being made by anyone in the movement, Dinesh knew, for the cadres never made any noise when they moved. There was a chance it was being made by a wounded person from the camp, though it would have been strange for a wounded person to have dragged themselves to the jungle instead of to the clinic or the hospital at this time of night, or, if they had been there for some time, to have started moaning now, when the last shelling had been early that morning. Whatever the source it made him suddenly nervous, for even if the sound didn't come from something dangerous the cadres would sooner or later hear it and be drawn into that section of the jungle to investigate, in which case they might come to the clearing too. If the voice was to stop relatively soon then maybe it made sense for them to take their chances waiting, lying there silently, but if on the other hand it was going to continue then probably it would be best to find out what it was as soon as possible to see if anything could be done. There was a chance that confronting the source of the sound could lead to some kind of commotion, they had no idea what was causing it after all, but if he were careful he could verify what it was while keeping his distance. Even if there was nothing they could do about it at least they would have some peace of mind, knowing what they were dealing with, rather than remaining anxious the rest of the night about what was making the sound and whether they were at risk. Perhaps, moreover, if Ganga saw that he was willing to go and investigate, she would realize that he was not helpless, that he was capable and that she could count on him. Perhaps she would forget about his having cried, or come to think of it as somehow exceptional, and perhaps by going Ganga's respect for him could even be restored. Dinesh sat up and looked at her. He hesitated at first, then tried to speak with confidence.

Why don't you wait here? I'll go and see what it is.

Ganga didn't say anything.

Don't worry if I don't return immediately, I'll be careful. I'll be back soon.

She motioned with her head to indicate that the idea was acceptable to her. There was an expression of slight relief on her face, less because the sound was bothering her, Dinesh couldn't help feeling, than because she wanted to be for a while on her own. It was only natural given what had happened though, and standing up Dinesh waited for the calling to start again so he could locate the direction it was coming from. When he was ready to leave he looked once more at Ganga, trying to smile with assurance, then began moving in slow, tentative steps, past the ferns and plants in front of the bed, into the heavy darkness beyond the trees. Clasping the branches and trunks for support he followed the rising and falling voice blindly, doing his best not to forget his position with respect to the clearing, since he was not on his usual path and it would be difficult to find his way back in the dark. In the short spells of silence he paused, gathered himself a little, and waited, and then, when the voice resumed, he recalibrated his path and continued forward. The sound became less dull and muted as he neared its point of origin, and rising and falling more rhythmically and distinctly in the air it began to seem more like a squawking or a hooting than anything intelligible, not like the sound of a human being at all, though beneath its harshness there was also an undertone of vulnerability, like the cries of an imperious child that didn't want to acknowledge its neediness. Dinesh slowed down as he got closer, his calves tensing as he moved uneasily on the tips of his toes, and entering at last the immediate vicinity of the sound he stopped and held back his breath, fearful of making his presence known. The sound rose up from a couple of meters in front of him, held itself aloft for a few seconds, and fell away. It was coming from a thicket of ferns clustered about the base of a tree, from somewhere inside the thicket, probably from under the cover of the fronds. Dinesh realized for the first time how small the source of the sound must be, probably some kind of small animal, smaller than a cat or dog, maybe even the size of a squirrel. He'd been nervous till then, not knowing what to expect, but letting out the air he was holding inside his chest he proceeded calmly and quickly now towards the thicket. The sound, which had just begun to rise up once more, broke off. Dinesh got down slowly on his knees, inserted his hands into the thicket, and cautiously, as though whatever was inside might bite, began sifting through the fronds. Almost at once he noticed the outlines of something hidden, and pushing the fronds to the side he leaned in. He brought his head close to the ground, squinted, and as his eyes became accustomed to the darkness he gradually began to see.

Sideways upon the earth, moist-eyed, unmoving, not quite a chick but not fully grown either, was a little black crow. Its curved black beak was half-open, frozen in the middle of its call, and its thin, twig-like black legs protruded out sideways from its body. Its small, undeveloped head was buried into its body at a strange angle, attached directly to the shoulders, as though its neck were broken or mutilated. The wing that was visible was damaged somehow too, wasn't properly tucked into the rest of the body, the ruffled feathers were no longer aligned with one another and were covered with a strange dark sheen, dried blood it seemed. On the earth just beneath its body glistened a

yellow-white substance, most likely shit. The crow must have been lying there a few hours at least. It was possible it had fallen from a tree
nearby during one of the bombings, though no shells had fallen recently in that part of the jungle. More probably it had been hurt by
one of the shells that had fallen in the camp that morning, and had
managed to fly towards the jungle before being forced by its injuries
to land. Dinesh parted the ferns around the crow more completely to
let in more light, and as he did so a fly took off from its wing. He waved
his hand over its body, and two more flies took flight. When he'd last
seen a bird Dinesh had no idea. He couldn't remember having seen a
single owl, heron, cuckoo, parrot or sparrow in the last months, not
even another crow, as though they'd all noticed the signs of war and
flown off long before, leaving only the confused or sick ones behind
with the evacuees, to be stunned into silence by the sound and heat of
the bombing.

Completely motionless on his knees Dinesh looked into the bird's
small, moist, perfectly round eye. Whether it was looking back at him
or not he couldn't tell but it let its beak close and began to make a sound.
Not the harsh high rising and falling of before but a soft, exhausted
wheezing, the sound of an old person rather than a child, as though
having attracted the attention of another living creature at last it could
stop calling out so loudly and insistently, be free, finally, to dwell ex-
clusively on its pain. Why it had expended so much effort calling out
to begin with, and what it thought another living creature could
do for it now, Dinesh couldn't say. He had no food to give it, no way to
treat or heal its wounds. He could only either put it out of its misery,
or simply let it be. If he killed it he could release it from this last stretch
of difficulty, while if he left it living it would have no choice but to wait,
would have to go on suffering till it died. Dinesh brought his face down

closer to the crow's ugly head and studied its curved black beak and small moist eye, its matted coat of black hair, and the light-pink skin that was visible underneath. If he wanted he could take the crow's hollow-boned little head between his thumb and forefinger and crush it, so completely that his fingertips met in the middle. He could crush the crow's skull so thoroughly that its life collapsed between his fingers, so that blood and brain matter trickled out through its beak, but though perhaps this was the kindest thing to do, there was no way he could bring himself to do it, Dinesh knew. He wanted to let the crow go on living, to let it continue existing, even if it was in pain and begging to be killed. Whether or not he killed it its time would come soon, and it might as well therefore have a little more time to experience and remember what living was like before it died. Dinesh freed his right hand of the fronds he was holding back, and with the tip of his index finger caressed the crow's head, which under the moist black hair was as hollow and fragile as an egg. Perhaps all it had wanted was company. Perhaps it had not wanted him to end its life at all, perhaps it had been calling out in the darkness just so that it could be for a while in the presence of someone else.

The crow blinked slowly and Dinesh caressed it once more, as if to reassure it that he would stay with it a while longer. Gently he let the remaining fronds return to their former position, so that the bird was once more inside the safety and security of the fern. Feeling out the ground behind him he let himself slowly drop backwards and lay down with his knees bent upwards, the tangle of grass, stems, leaves and earth soft beneath his back and head. He couldn't keep Ganga waiting too long of course, for if he took too much time she might think something had happened and leave the clearing in search of him. All the same there was probably no harm in lying there beside the crow for just a few more minutes, not just to give it the small solace of another living creature's presence, but also because if he left immediately there was a chance it would notice and begin calling out loudly once more. If he stayed for a while then maybe, having been sufficiently calmed by his brief presence, the crow would remain silent when he left. It felt pleasant, in any case, just to lie there next to it, in the unknown darkness of that new part of the jungle. It felt like a sanctuary, like a place he could collect himself after having spent so much time crying uncontrollably on Ganga's shoulder. The echoes of his convulsions were still aching softly inside him, and lying there for a while on the tender earth he could wait and listen as they quietened, as his body began to contain them more fully and wholly, so that he would be composed when afterwards he returned to the clearing and lay down once more beside Ganga.

One afternoon or evening long before, he must have been thirteen or fourteen years old, studying in the main room of the house at the desk his brother had used for his studies before leaving school to join the movement, he had turned to look at the clock on the opposite wall and noticed, through the corner of his eye, a gecko by the foot of the table. It was a little unusual to see a gecko sitting on the ground like that in the daytime but he returned to his work without paying any attention to it, he had been studying for end-of-year exams at the time, and was caught up in the practice problems he was working on. An hour or so later however, leaning back against his chair to take a break from the exercise book he had been writing in for so long, he looked down and saw that the gecko was still there, in exactly the same place he had seen it earlier. It was bigger than ordinary, about as long as his index finger, and its legs and abdomen were thick and fleshy, its eyes black and bulbous in its calm, triangular face. He clapped his hands to shoo it away, but it remained calmly where it was. He lifted up the back legs of his plastic chair and dropped them back on the cement floor so they clattered loudly, but the gecko remained perfectly still beside the leg of the table. Lifting his legs up from the ground Dinesh leaned down towards it and clicked his fingers above its head to try to scare it away. Its eyes widened, but for some reason the gecko refused to move. Its abdomen was expanding and contracting rapidly, and beneath its translucent beige skin faint blue pulses of blood were flashing quickly through its body. Unsure what was going on Dinesh took his pencil, drew back his chair, and kneeled down on the floor well behind the gecko. He tapped the eraser end of the pencil on the floor a few inches behind the tail, but nothing happened. Slowly he brought the pencil closer and closer, till he was tapping the floor a half centimeter behind its back legs, and finally he lifted the pencil up and cautiously, firmly though not heavily, prodded the gecko's back. The eraser sank into its soft, almost elastic body and the gecko made a sudden jerk, attempted to scuttle away and in the process twisted one of its back legs strangely under its body and froze again. It remained like that till he touched it again and the other three legs started scrambling hard against the floor. They dragged its body and the twisted leg a short way, but gave up when it had moved less than two inches from its previous spot. The gecko had been hurt or injured somehow apparently. Its back left leg couldn't move and without it neither could the gecko. How it had gotten to its place by the foot of the table was hard to say, but there was no way it would be able to move from there by itself. Dinesh drew a little closer to the injured animal, brought down his head a little lower, and looked at the lifeless limb, which had returned inadvertently to its normal position in the last series of movements. The limb seemed no different from the other three;

it stretched out from the gecko's soft milky body and terminated in a small, pad-like foot, out of which five tiny rounded toes poked, all of them the same length, less than a millimeter long, each one so soft and so delicate it seemed impossible to replace.

Dinesh had tried going back to work, but found it hard to concentrate knowing that the gecko was lying there incapacitated on the floor. It would remain right there beside him if he did nothing he knew and the thought upset him, not merely upset but nauseated him. The gecko was so soft, so vulnerable, its large unblinking eyes so desperate. Its strong, substantial body was the picture of vitality so long as it kept still, but because of its invisibly maimed leg even its healthy limbs had become obsolete, leaving it unable to perform the most rudimentary functions. It was as though it hoped that by not moving a muscle it could persuade potential predators that it was healthy, that there was no point coming after it, although at the same time of course it must have known that it would have to submit passively to whatever happened to it. Unable to tolerate the situation any longer Dinesh drew back his chair. He flipped to the back of his exercise book, tore out a used piece of lined paper, and got on his knees. Nudging the gecko with the pencil he forced it onto the paper, then holding the paper cautiously by both edges in case it attempted to move he stood up slowly, walked outside—aware all the while of the large gecko's weight in the center of the paper—and deposited it upside down in the grass near the far corner of the garden. He turned around and walked back quickly to the house. It was difficult knowing as he sat back down at his desk that the gecko would be torn apart soon by a rat or by a crow, that as a result of what he'd done it would have to watch without comment as its soft body was ripped open by a beak or claws. If he'd done nothing it would have had his protection while he studied at least, the protection of the house too, but sooner or later obviously it would have had to meet the same fate, sooner or later some creature or other would have found it there by the foot of the table and pounced on it. It was still alive he knew, it would take some time for it to be found lying there helplessly in the grass, but knowing that it was about to die was easier at least to endure than the idea of it continuing to live in its pathetic state.

The two situations must have been different in some subtle way, for unlike the gecko it didn't bother Dinesh at all now to remain beside the wounded crow. He didn't feel the urge to end its existence or to move away from its presence and in fact he was even calmed by the crow, comforted by its nearness. Perhaps it was the desperation in the gecko's unblinking eyes and rapidly throbbing abdomen that had made the gecko so difficult to be next to, a desperation that was less prominent in the crow, or perhaps, on reflection more likely in fact, the two situations were actually more or less the same, and it was simply he who had changed. Whatever the case Dinesh was glad knowing that the crow was alive there beneath the fronds, that it would remain there for at least a while after he returned to the clearing, and that it would have the opportunity to spend this time in the body it had been with for so long. He wanted it to think of its life even if it was suffering, for it to be alone in the presence of itself in ways that might have eluded it before. And even if the crow had done so already, even if that was how the crow had spent all its time since it had fallen from the sky out of exhaustion, there was no harm, he felt, if it continued doing so for just a little longer.

Dinesh stretched his arms out and yawned silently. Crying had exhausted him, and if he lay there much longer there was a risk that he could fall asleep. He got to his feet sluggishly, and remaining still for a while as the daze from standing up evened out, stretched his arms out and yawned once more. His eyelids were heavy and slightly swollen but the rest of him felt surprisingly light, as though having emptied, through his tears, the deep wells of water that had amassed behind his eyes, his body had now lost most of its weight. Dinesh looked at the fern under which the crow was lying, then moved quietly towards a tree a few feet beside it. He pulled up his sarong with his left hand and held his penis aloft with the other. It still felt small, incapable of becoming heavier or harder, but concentrating for a moment with his eyes closed he strained, and from it emerged a little trickle. Straining harder he opened his eyes and watched as a long, soundless stream vaulted up, carved an arc through the air and then pattered heavily on the bark and the leaves of the plants at the base of the tree. He directed the stream gently with his hand from left to right, listened with satisfaction to the variations of the patter as it fell on different kinds of leaves, then guiding it upwards strained harder to see how high and far he could make it go. He pushed for as long as he could but gradually the arc began to diminish, its height and length lessened, it forked briefly into two thinner streams and then dwindled finally into a single drip. Dinesh shook himself off and retied his sarong. He looked back towards the fern as though to inform the crow that he was leaving, a little regretful, but glad he was able to leave behind something of himself to keep it company.

It was easier to find his way back than he'd worried, and moving silently beneath the lightless canopy Dinesh began to feel strangely calm, peaceful in a way that he hadn't for some time. It was as though he contained something valuable inside him, as though an airtight space inside his rib cage were sheltering some small, fragile item, something so precious that the rest of his body, his eyes and ears and his hands and feet, existed only in order to sustain it. All the possibilities he needed were contained inside this thing, he felt, and by means of it he had become autonomous and self-sustaining, independent, somehow, of the world outside him, more and more with every step he took towards the clearing. It was true that he and Ganga had not been able to make love, that he had disappointed her probably by crying, but they were married now, were part of each other's lives, and in some ways at least she seemed to like him. Probably she would continue to like him despite what had happened, and if so then most likely they would have a chance to make love again in the future too, maybe on the following night, and if not maybe on one of the nights after. They hadn't been able to sustain the union that had formed briefly between them through speaking, but they would have a chance to speak again the next day too, if not maybe in the days after, and in the future they would have the chance to create habits that would let them live together in the same world without even having to speak. There was a chance, of course, that one or even both of them would be killed before the end of the war, but there was a chance too that they would both survive. It was possible that one or both of them would be injured, that one or both of them would have to live with an amputated arm or an amputated leg, but it was possible too that they would both be able to escape whole and unharmed, physically at least. In either case they could live together, they could find some kind of work and sleep in the same place together, they could lie beside one another and be with each other. There was no guarantee that things would end like this, there was no way to be totally sure, but whatever the situation and whatever the likelihood Dinesh couldn't help feeling that all he needed was safe within his chest, that everything that mattered was sealed inside his body, and that there was no longer anything he needed to worry about.

When he arrived at the edge of the clearing Ganga was on her knees at the edge of the bed, leaning over the beige bag and looking carefully through its contents, searching for something apparently. She stopped what she was doing when she heard his footsteps over the plants and ferns, and looking up watched Dinesh inquiringly as he made his way to the bed. He was curious to know what she'd been looking for in the bag, but he hesitated for a moment and Ganga spoke before he could ask.

What happened?

It was only a crow, said Dinesh quietly, as he took off his slippers and kneeled down on the sari next to the earthen pillow. It was wounded somehow, that's why it was shouting. I think its wing was probably injured in the shelling.

I thought it must have been some kind of animal. What did you do?

Nothing. When I got there it stopped crying on its own.

What took so long then?

I thought I should probably wait there for a while, to make sure it didn't start shouting again. Why? Were you worried that something happened?

Ganga studied him, though what she was thinking it was difficult to say. She shook her head. No. I was just wondering what was taking so long. I noticed when the sound stopped, and thought you'd be back straight after.

Nothing happened. I wanted to make sure it wouldn't start again, so I sat down on the ground next to it. I thought that maybe it just wanted some company, and that if I stayed with it for a while it wouldn't start shouting again when I left.

Ganga gazed down at her lap. She looked up at him again after a while then spoke, her voice soft but even. If its wing was hurt, it probably would have been better just to kill it. Birds don't usually survive if they aren't able to fly.

I thought about it, said Dinesh, shifting his body slightly. I didn't want to, I don't know why. Not that I was scared. I would have done it if I had to, if it hadn't stopped making noise. I just felt it might as well stay alive for a little longer, if it was going to die soon anyway.

Ganga regarded him as he said this, then shook her head as if to say that she felt differently, but that probably nothing would be gained by discussing the issue further. She gazed down in silence at her hands for a while, then turned towards the beige bag, which was still open, and began rearranging a few of the things inside. There was no indication in anything she said or did, Dinesh felt, that she was still dwelling on the fact that he'd cried. The only change he could sense was that she sounded more patient now than when they had talked before, not necessarily less reserved, but gentler, as though she had decided, while he was gone, to be less severe with him, as though it was she who needed to look after him and not the other way around. She quietly zipped the bag shut and moved back towards the rock, where stretching out her legs and reclining backwards, she lay down on the sari, and stared up at the small opening of dark-blue sky above. He still wanted to ask her what she'd been looking for in the bag, before he arrived, but she looked as though she was deeply immersed in thought, and Dinesh could sense that she didn't want to be disturbed. He continued watching her for a while without moving, then stretching himself out along his side of the bed, lay down so that he was parallel to her, their bodies close but not touching, the airy fabric of the sari beneath him cool on the moist skin of his legs. In the darkness above he could make out the outlines of the leaves and branches, and through the gap between them, the same section of sky that Ganga was lost in.

Breathing out, Dinesh let his head fall back and his body slacken. He felt unworried now, for the first time since they'd gotten married, about the prospect of being together in silence. He still felt peacefully inside himself, and though he would have been glad to know what Ganga was thinking, the effort required to keep himself at the surface of his existence, to exist at the level of his lips and fingertips, seemed unnecessary now. He was even more tired than earlier, and his body had begun to feel heavy, his head most of all. What he wanted above all was to lie down flat on the ground, and let himself sink head-first into the earth. It wasn't urgent or vital that he and Ganga talk or interact, there was no longer any need for them to be always engaging, as if failure to do so would mean coming apart. They were married now. There would be more chances to talk, to understand and get closer to each other, there would be time in the future to show her that she could trust him to support her. Dinesh took in a deep breath, and listened as his chest rose softly and fell. Beside him Ganga's chest also rose and fell, with its own rhythm, but without being in conflict with his, weaving peacefully in and out of his in the warm, patient silence that ensconced them. Unlike the intimate silence in which they'd come together earlier, which was fragile and took great effort to sustain, unlike the tense silence in which they'd stood next to each other after getting married, when the strange new presence of another body made withdrawal into oneself impossible, the silence that surrounded them now felt different somehow, less demanding. It was the silence that belonged to people who had grown to some degree accustomed to each other, who had learned how to be in physical proximity and yet remain in their own worlds, to preserve their own moods in the presence of one another. Dinesh felt glad to let this new silence continue undisturbed, and closing his eyes he simply listened as the air entered his nose and filled up his chest, as it ebbed back into the atmosphere and emptied out from his chest.

It was difficult of course to know what he and Ganga would do in the future, how they would spend their time together. People in the camp neither talked nor did anything else in their free time, it was true, but people in general did do things with their time, Dinesh knew, they spent their days doing things both by themselves and with others. Scattered images appeared in his mind of the Jaffna town that he had visited as a child, before the government had taken over the peninsula and they'd been forced to make the long exodus to the mainland. He could see all the smartly dressed people on the streets, walking, talking, and shopping, riding cycles, catching buses, and clutching their bags, moving always with quick, purposeful strides. In ordinary life people were always carrying things, it seemed. It hadn't seemed unusual or surprising to him as a child, he'd taken it for granted and as a result had never stopped to reflect on it, but thinking back on it now it was hard to know what exactly people had always been so busy carrying. Umbrellas, maybe, if it was raining, handkerchiefs, if they were sick. Newspapers, maybe, so they could read something as they were waiting, so they could know what everybody else in the world was doing. Schoolchildren had to carry their books of course, their pencils and erasers, and then most people took a little money with them wherever they went, so they had to carry purses and wallets, and also anything that they bought with the money they took. People were always buying things after all, that was why in the town there had been so many shops and stalls. They needed food to eat, and so they bought vegetables and meat, sweets too, if they liked sweets. They had to buy wood or gas for cooking, and clothes to wear, medicine and brooms, things for the kitchen, anything that was necessary for the upkeep of their homes. Dinesh tried to think of all those people going busily about their business, doing whatever they had to do, carrying with them all they would need during the course of the day, as well as anything they needed to take back later to their homes. There was so much activity in the scenes he remembered, so much movement, always so many people coming and going, on buses and bicycles, by train and by foot, so much that there was still something slightly difficult for him to comprehend. Where were they all coming from and where were they going, and why always with such urgency? It was difficult to say in general, naturally, since it depended on the particular person, on how they earned a living, and who they spent time with, and it depended also on the time of day and the day of the week. Wherever they were headed in particular, though, in a general sense people were always either moving towards their homes or away, either directly or by means of intermediate destinations. They were drawn towards their homes when they were outside, but they were also always drawn away from them when they were inside, for no matter how important it seemed to its occupants wasn't a home, after all, just a temporary abode, a place a person could eat, rest, and sleep, where they could store securely all the things they needed for life so they didn't have to start from scratch the next day? No matter how central or stable it felt a home was only a provisional place of rest in the longer course of movement that started at birth and ended in death, and why this movement was so important, why people continued moving despite all the obstacles they faced, it was hard to say.

A wave of cool air washed over Dinesh, cooled his skin, and receded. His chest rose and fell as he gazed up through the canopy into
the sky, slowly rose and slowly fell, the air softly advancing and receding. Perhaps people simply had no choice. Perhaps they had to keep
moving, to get up in the morning, and to go on until evening. Breathing was not a choice or habit after all, it was not something you could
start or stop at will. The atmosphere entered the body of its own accord, and in the same way it took its leave, from the first breath to the
last, and so perhaps in a way living was not a choice. The air would
go on advancing, and till it stopped it would go on receding. When
you were hungry you would have to eat, and when you were thirsty
you would have to drink. When your bladder was full you would
have to piss, and when your bowels were full you would have to shit.
The legs had to move, and so people had to go places, and so there
were places they went. The arms had to work too, and so people had to
carry things, and so there were things they gripped and held. All the
while the atmosphere kept advancing and receding, the chest kept rising and falling, and maybe that was all, maybe that was life. If you had
no food you would no longer be able to eat, and if you didn't eat you'd
no longer have to shit. If you had no water you would no longer be
able to drink, and if you didn't drink you'd no longer have to piss. If
your legs had been ruptured, or punctured, or blown away, you no
longer had to walk, and the same went for the arms. All it meant was
less work to do as you kept living, as the atmosphere kept entering and
kept leaving, advancing into the body and then receding, as the chest
kept rising, and falling, and rising, and falling, until at last that stilled
too, and perhaps that, when it happened, was simply that.

Dinesh turned slowly onto his side so that he was facing outwards,
his back towards Ganga, who had already turned so that she was fac-

ing the rock. His leaden eyelids were closing over his tired, burning eyes, and his head felt heavy upon the earth. Careful not to take up too much space on the bed, he bent his legs a little and curled up his body, shuffled backwards a little towards Ganga, inched closer to her warmth and softness, so that her back was pressed lightly against his, so that her heels lay against his calves. Breathing silently in and silently out, curling up his body and hunching in his shoulders and head, Dinesh felt a long, wide fatigue sweeping over him, washing over his loosened limbs. Falling asleep was, in a way, the closest a person could come to renouncing the world outside them while still alive, and it was a strange thing therefore that in order to sleep one still needed to be in a safe and comforting place, one needed something reliable in the outside world to be able to hold on to or at least to touch, like an anchored boat to which a diver is attached as he descends into the sea, reassured that there is something on the surface that he can return to when the time comes. Dinesh slipped his left hand under his head and shuffled back just a little more, so that he could feel Ganga's warm, living presence just a little more fully upon his back, and feeling this safety and comfort for the first time in how long he couldn't say, he drifted, slowly, into a state of deep and silent sleep.

8

A SOUND CAME TO HIM from deep inside the earth, a deep, gentle reverberation, and as though the earth were calling out to him from below Dinesh curled his body up into a tighter ball. He hunched his shoulders, drew in his legs, and with the hand that lay between his head and the earthen pillow clasped the ground as though to be in contact with it more intimately. His body tensed, then relaxed, and the calm unknowingness of his face remained undisturbed. There was quiet for a while and then, louder and less gently, the reverberation sounded once more, not just beneath him this time but also above and around. His body tensed again, his hand gripped the pillow more tightly, and as though some part of him sensed now that the world was trying to pry him away from his peaceful sleep, he hunched his shoulders once more, and drew in his knees to his chest. He furrowed his eyebrows, screwed up his eyelids, did his best to insulate himself from everything outside that was trying to penetrate in but found himself suspended instead between sleeping and waking, in that strange, liminal state when one was with oneself in a way one was not at any other time, when in the dark seed of consciousness the questions and complexities of life were crystallized into a simple choice between waking up and staying asleep, between rejoining the world and staying withdrawn, though in a way of course the choice was not really a choice since sooner or later one had to wake up anyway, sooner or later light, noise, hunger, or the need to piss forced one to get up and rejoin. Tucking his head into his body and knotting his forehead in concentration Dinesh tried to insinuate himself back into his state of unconsciousness, to postpone making the choice he was being presented with, but somewhere in the distance he heard a light whispering of air, a faraway whooshing that turned slowly into a whistling, as of something smooth and heavy dropping down through the sky, and the pitch of this whistling getting higher he felt himself falling as if the earth below him had given way, dropping back headfirst through the darkness while the whistling grew higher and more piercing till all at once it came to a stop. The choice, it seemed, had been made for him. Like a bucket long immersed inside a well that is yanked up suddenly by its rope, he opened his eyes. In the distance there was a loud, expansive explosion.

It was pitch black, and a wide, penetrating silence surrounded him. Dinesh remained in his sleeping position, slightly confused, and slowly the distant edges of the silence were pierced by the wailing of muted human voices. He turned to his side, and raising his head leaned on his elbow. His eyes were swollen, his head like heavy, fractured glass. He wanted to lie back down and close his eyes but knew that something was happening that he needed to pay attention to. He rubbed his eyes and drew his hand through his hair, then remembering that he was married turned over to look at Ganga, who was not there. He was lying in the middle of the bed and Ganga was not there between him and the rock as she had been when they went to bed, the sari's folds on her side of the bed were continuous with those on his, as if nobody had lain next to him at all. Once more from the direction of the camp there came a whistling, higher and more distinct than before. It was followed by several others, each one laid over the preceding ones, then by explosions, each louder and more sweeping than the one before, in the camp still but much closer now to their section of the jungle. Dinesh sat up and looked around uneasily. The clearing was filled with the almost complete darkness that preceded dawn, but he could make out the water bottle still there next to the rock, the pots and pans and the beige bag by the foot of the bed. He began to feel an uncomfortable pounding in the lower part of his chest. He got onto his knees and looked along the border of the bed for Ganga's slippers, and failing to find them stood up quickly and stumbled backwards with dizziness till he caught hold of the rock for support. Leaning on it with both hands he tried to steady himself. He waited to make sure he was capable of standing, then straightening up looked around the clearing again with deliberate slowness, as if it was only out of some inexplicable inattentiveness that he was failing to see Ganga. He did his best to stay calm. Getting onto his knees he patted with the palm of his hands the section of sari on which she had been lying earlier, to confirm with his hands what his eyes were seeing. It was possible of course that she had only needed to go to the bathroom and that soon she would be back, or that maybe she'd just felt like going out for a brief walk. It was possible that leaving the clearing in search of her would only succeed in separating them for good, that the best thing to do was simply stay put till she returned to the clearing by herself, but remembering then in the stupor of having just woken up how he'd

cried before they went to bed, how uncertain Ganga had been about
how to respond and how afterwards she had wanted to be alone and
silent so she could think her own thoughts, Dinesh became certain,
suddenly, that she'd gone back to the camp.

Dinesh got slowly to his feet. He stood still for a moment till he
was steady, then clenching his jaw and tensing his body began to run
as fast as he could. Trampling the plants and ferns between the bed
and the edge of the clearing he made his way into the jungle without
turning back, though no sooner had he entered it than the density of
vegetation and the darkness forced him to slow down, to raise and place
his feet carefully to avoid tripping on the plants and knotted roots.
He felt much worse physically than he had before going to bed, as if
having slept properly for a few hours for the first time in months, his
body had become aware suddenly of how deprived it was of sleep. His
head swayed heavily from side to side, his joints were stiff, and grasp-
ing blindly at the branches and trunks for support he moved as if for
the first time after having been sick for days in bed. He made his way
through the trees, however, and his balance slowly began to improve,
his legs becoming more stable and more capable of carrying his
weight. With each of the shells that fell in the distance his daze too
was lifted a little further, as though with each boom some of the dense,
heavy clutter in his mind was razed, leaving flat open space in which
he could think. Most likely Ganga had gone back to the camp in search
of her father. It was the first night she'd been separated from him, and
probably she'd wanted to go back to the tent to make sure that he was
okay. She'd heard the shelling in the camp probably, started to worry
about him, and had left intending to return to the clearing right afterwards, unless she'd left before the shelling had started, which made
sense actually since he himself had probably woken up as soon as the

first shell had fallen, and would have seen her as she was leaving if that was when she had left. Most likely she hadn't been able to fall asleep, she'd said after all that once she woke she could never go back to bed, and lying awake in the silence, remembering that her father had been absent when they went back to the tent for dinner, most likely she'd felt the urge to go back and check whether he'd returned yet, whether he was sleeping there and whether he'd eaten the food she'd left. Unless of course she'd come to realize that her father probably wasn't planning to return to the tent at all, that probably he'd abandoned her for good, in which case there must have been another reason she'd decided to go back to the camp. Maybe she'd been upset by the way he'd cried, had felt that he was weak or helpless and that she was better off alone, though surely that couldn't have been the reason either, since surely he'd proven to her that he could be counted on at least to a degree, when he'd left the clearing despite the obvious danger to investigate the source of the threatening sounds. Maybe she'd just gone back to the camp to get something she'd left behind, some money or some food or an item of clothing. It was hard to say, but in any case it was probably best not to think about it too much, Dinesh knew. The main thing was to find her and make sure she was safe, he could dwell on why she'd left later if he liked, when they were together again and when there was time.

Dinesh looked up and saw that he'd come without realizing it to the edge of the camp. He continued walking forward, slowed down a bit, then after a few steps came to a stop. Thick, seething clouds of smoke were billowing up into the blue-black dawn sky, shrouding large sections of the camp in dark gray. From what he could make out there were two or three fires close to the center of the camp, what was burning he couldn't say, and not far south of where he stood two tents

near the camp's edge were ablaze too. Beside them a still-rooted coconut tree had snapped in two, its fronds writhing on the ground
around it like burning hair, its coconuts scattered like heads across the
rubble. From all over the camp rose piercing shouts and screams, and
from sections of jungle around the camp the muted bursts of the movement's small, portable mortars could be heard. Dinesh stood there for
a while, unmoving. He had known the camp was being shelled, obviously, for he'd heard the explosions and the wailing in the clearing and
on his way through the jungle, but it was only now, when what he had
been hearing was spread out visibly before him, that he consciously
registered the fact that not merely had Ganga left the clearing but that
she was also, if she was indeed in the camp, vulnerable to the shelling.
Dinesh stumbled forward a few steps. He picked up a little speed, then
suddenly began to run. He moved as fast as he could in the southwesterly direction of Ganga's tent but before he'd even passed the outskirts of the camp there came from overhead a whistling, the sound of
heavy metal hurtling through the sky, and he dropped down flat on
the barely visible earth, his eyes pressed down over his knuckles. The
shell exploded some distance to the west, in the general vicinity of
the clinic. It was too far away to have to worry about shrapnel but
he waited for a moment just to make sure, then looked up and saw
clouds of dust and smoke rising in the distance. Just as he was getting
up another shell exploded near the first, this one unheralded by any
whistling, and he fell back upon the ground with his face to the earth.
He waited again, stood up, and continued moving. He ran as fast as
he could through the mostly empty periphery of the camp, but slowed
down again as he made his way into the more populated parts, into
the increasing density of people and things. Everywhere there was
howling, wailing, shouting and screaming, and all he could make out

in the semidarkness were sweating bodies, clutching hands, stamping feet and contorted mouths. The corrugated steel and palm leaf covers had already been drawn over a few of the bunkers but most of the evacuees were still above ground, pushing frantically past each other in different directions, some in search of relatives, some for the best place to take cover, others seemingly because they did not know what else to do. Dinesh slowed down a bit and tried to gather his bearings, to think for a minute just to make sure he had chosen the most sensible course of action. He wasn't yet near Ganga's tent but there a chance, he knew, that having heard the shelling she might decide to leave the tent and return to the clearing, in which case they might pass one another without realizing, he on his way to the tent and she on her way back. Looking around Dinesh tried to identify the faces of the people running by, but he was unable to break into the continuous mass of motion that surrounded him. His eyes came to rest on the only person in the area who remained completely still, a small boy standing motionlessly in front of a tent, obscured except for brief glimpses by all the people hurrying past. He was eight or nine years old probably, shirtless in a pair of dirty blue shorts. He stood there gazing thoughtfully into some indeterminate point on the ground before him, eyes wide like empty black saucers, as if dwelling on something other than the situation around him.

A shell fell to the south, and Dinesh resumed running. Another fell behind him to the north, in the section of jungle close to the clearing, but he couldn't stop to look for he knew his best chance was to get to Ganga's tent as soon as possible. Most likely she would stay in the cover of the tent's dugout until the shelling was over, most likely she would stay put and he would be able to find her there, but just in case she was considering leaving for the clearing in the midst of everything he needed to get there as soon as possible, or there was a chance they would miss each other. He moved as fast as his tired legs would allow, his chest heaving since he was weak and hadn't run so much in a long time. Rising up in the background of his panting there came another whistling, higher and more distinct than the earlier ones. Dinesh dropped to the dusty ground, hid his face in his hands, closed his eyes, and waited. He heard voices nearby, a woman and a man calling, and glancing quickly to his right saw two faces looking out from under the corrugated steel covering of a bunker, beckoning him to get in. It seemed like maybe they recognized him, it was difficult to say for sure, but he had no idea who they were and couldn't afford to go inside anyway, he had to get to Ganga as soon as he could. If she was still in the tent when he got there they would be able to take cover in the bunker together he knew, holding each other tightly till the trembling of the earth gave way to silence. They would be able to put their arms around each other and breathe together, comfort each other, and even if a shell fell near them it wouldn't matter since sheltering in the same bunker meant that if one of them died then probably so would the other, that they'd have the opportunity to die together in a small and private space. If one of them was wounded it would be a different story of course, but if it was her then he would take care of her as best he could, push her wheelchair and bathe her and whatever else she needed, unless they were both wounded in which case perhaps they would have all the more reason to live together, so that each of them could compensate for the inabilities and incapacities of the other.

The shell exploded to the south, so loud it almost couldn't be heard. The ground reverberated heavily, and clouds of scorching dust, thick and pungent, rose up into the air. Dinesh stayed down, eyes closed as heavy shards of shrapnel tore tight lines through the air, then hearing the screaming of someone to his left he opened his eyes and turned around, squinting through a slit between his fingers to see what had happened. An old man was lying on the ground with half his right leg severed. The knee was bleeding profusely, and the man was screaming not so much in pain it seemed as in disbelief at what had happened. Dinesh stood up shakily and tried to get his bearings. It was difficult to say where he was suddenly, he felt strangely dazed. Looking ahead he saw heavy smoke not so far away, coming from one of the clinic buildings that was apparently completely in flames, not the staff building but the main one, the one with all the classrooms, which meant he needed to continue in more or less the same general direction though a little more to the south in order to get to the vicinity of the tent. He turned and was about to resume moving when the screaming beside him turned into a strange mixture of gasping and gargling, and looking back he saw that the old man was scraping up clumps of earth from the ground with both hands, trying to stop the blood by sprinkling it evenly over his overflowing stump. Dinesh tried to run as fast he could, but somehow everything seemed to slow down, as in a dream in which one needs to scramble quickly to escape something but can, for some reason, move only in slow motion. The ground beneath him was scorched black, and through the rubber of his slippers he could feel its heat. The air was thick with smoke and sulfur, impossible almost to breathe, and the outlines of everything seemed strangely warped—the singed skin and hair of a body, the glistening plastic of melting tents—everything deformed by the vapor and heat, assuming the distorted clarity of things seen through a concave lens. Except for bags, pots, bottles, and other things that were strewn across the ground, lost or left out in the rush, the camp seemed suddenly devoid of human life. Except for those who'd been killed or wounded and the people who were sitting beside them in bewilderment, almost all the evacuees were inside dugouts it seemed. Dinesh passed a man who was carrying a small boy limp in his arms, the man in his mid-forties, the boy twelve or thirteen, his son most likely. He carried the boy a few feet in one direction, turned abruptly and walked a few feet the opposite way, then not quite sure where to go with the dead child stopped and looked at Dinesh as if for directions. Dinesh kept moving, doing his best to keep his eyes trained as far as possible into the distance. He passed a woman kneeling on the ground before the body of a young girl. With the conviction of a mother who knows how to make her child behave the woman was hammering the girl's chest with her fists, as though by thumping hard enough her child would be compelled to respond out of fear or guilt. The woman's eyes were large and swollen, her jaw unhinged and the veins in her neck bulging, and unable to stop himself from coming to a pause in front of her Dinesh realized that though she was screaming without restraint no sound was coming from her mouth, that in fact no sound was coming from anything at all. The world around him, he realized, was entirely mute. How long it had been that way was hard to say. Perhaps he'd been unable to hear for some time, imagining that people were shouting when really he was only inferring so from the looks on their faces, that he could hear shells exploding when really he could only tell by the shaking of the ground below his feet and the waves of hot, surging air that blew past him. Dinesh looked up, tried to absorb the silence all around him, and all at once felt, or perhaps just tried to feel, a sense of calm.

He resumed moving, neither fast nor slow. The ground under his feet slowly became less hot, the smoke less thick as he made his way south, into a section of the camp that was apparently still unshelled. He was nearing the vicinity of Ganga's tent it was clear, everything was vaguely familiar, the orderliness of the tents, the locations of the uncovered bunkers, his distance and bearing from the still burning clinic, and then not far ahead of him he recognized, by its size and the way the blue tarpaulin sagged between the poles, the rear of Ganga's tent. There was little chance he would find her inside he suddenly felt sure, probably she'd left for the clearing as soon as the shelling had started, or had never even come back to the camp at all, but all the same he felt a nervous tension in his body as he got closer, as if his feet wanted to remain where they were but an invisible steel wire attached to his chest, suspending him in the air, was pulling him onward. Despite the hesitation in his body he felt himself drawn soundlessly around the back of the tent, past the little pit in which they'd cooked rice the evening before, which contained still all the cinders and charred black pieces of wood from the fire, round to the front of the tent where Ganga was lying on her stomach a few feet from the entrance, her arms stretched out in front of her. Her feet were crossed at a strange angle, and her pink frock was drawn up above her knees, leaving bare the coffee-colored skin of her lower thighs and calves. She was facing away, and taking care to keep his distance, as though to respect her privacy as much as possible, Dinesh circled round silently so that he could see her face. The right side of her head, which seemed somewhat swollen, was pressed upon the ground. Her left eye was half-open and the right corner of her parted lips was kissing the dirt. Pooled thickly under her waist was blood, not much but more than enough, and quietly, as though the wire holding him up was being gently lowered, Dinesh sank to his knees. The ground beneath him was quivering. The air felt too warm and heavy to breathe. He ran his hands through his hair, which was thicker and drier now that it had been washed and soaped, then ran them over the top of his thighs, over his newly clean sarong. Inside his chest there was a tightening, the sensation of air beginning to recede, and he wrapped his arms tightly around his torso as if for support. The air in his chest continued receding, and trying to fight off the sensation of choking that came over him he leaned forward onto both hands, brought his face down to the ground in front of him, and retched, heaved. Nothing came up. He brushed away the earth that clung to his moist forehead and tried to lift up his head but the air inside him continued escaping and unable to look up he retched, again, heaved, as though there was something stuck between his chest and the bottom of his throat that was refusing to emerge. He stroked the ground pleadingly with both hands, did his best to take air into his lungs, to tense his body and hold his diaphragm steady, but despite his best efforts his chest continued buckling, and casting about for something to hold on to and finding nothing, like a person falling in the darkness who expects at every moment to hit the ground but who instead just goes on falling, he fell quietly upon his side where he remained, except for his silent gagging, completely still.

What happens, at such times, it is difficult to know. There were moments, in the course of ordinary life, in which one breathed in more fully, when with a strange clarity one felt it was possible to move beyond the limits of daily existence, that simply by inhaling one could draw the world into one's body and contain within one's skin its expanses, wholly and permanently. And perhaps, if such moments existed, it made sense to think there were moments also in which one breathed out more or less fully, in which one's chest contracted and one was forced to watch as the air in one's lungs receded, as it was drawn back out by the atmosphere and one's self as a consequence dwindled, diminished to a point so small that soon, one felt, one would dissolve into the world beyond one's skin. Perhaps, though every single moment of being alive consisted of breathing, in and out, and in and out, never once ceasing since breathing of course occurred independently of choice or habit, was a pact between the chest and the atmosphere about which the mind could say nothing, perhaps, though life itself was nothing but an oscillation between these states, between drawing in the atmosphere and having it drawn back out, between attempting unconsciously to encompass the world and then being forced to give it all up, perhaps it was only in these rare moments of more complete inhalation or exhalation that the relationship between oneself and the world one had always been breathing became explicit, in which one really saw the limits of encompassment and dissolution between which one had always been oscillating, from one's painful first breath at birth, which was the greatest attempt at incorporating what was outside, to one's weary last breath at death, when one was swept completely out of one's body, and lost at last in the atmosphere. It was hard to know what exactly was happening as the air inside Dinesh's lungs continued to empty and his chest contracted to the point of almost collapsing, as the ground beneath him reverberated without pause and as with glazed, unfocused eyes he stared sideways at Ganga's body, but perhaps what Dinesh was dwelling on as he lay there without moving was this above all, that he contained inside him less of the world than he had at any other point in his life, that the air he was losing, no matter how strenuously he attempted to breathe it back in subsequently, would most likely not be replaced, and that though of course his chest would retain some air as long as he continued living its capacity for containing air was now being diminished for good, so that like an old man or invalid he would be capable from then on of taking only small, cautious sips of the atmosphere, till he died and was at last permitted to fully dissolve.

Dinesh closed his eyes and tried getting up but couldn't, was unable to properly summon the effort. He turned over onto his back and tried again to raise his torso but was again unable, his strength having dissipated so widely across his body that it couldn't be focused into specific movements. He let his head fall back upon the ground, and lying there supine, parallel to Ganga, gazed up limply at the thick diffusion of smoke and dust above him. It was well past dawn but the day's light was blunted by the masses of black cloud. They had spread out as far as he could see across the camp, spiraling upwards heavily where shells had just fallen and where things were burning, just thin enough at points to give glimpses of the colorless sky beyond. Dinesh closed his eyes again and tried to focus, as if he needed to do something before the air remaining in his body was lost and he was rendered helpless. Straining his upper body as much as he could he tried again to raise himself up from the ground, and successful this time, he sat up and attempted to collect himself. Trying to come to some kind of understanding of the situation he looked again at Ganga, focusing not on her half-open eye or the blood that had pooled out from under her stomach but simply on the fact that she was lying there unmoving beside him, unmoving but more or less whole. He felt an urge to put his arms around her, to grab her and hold her tightly and keep her pressed to him, to do something to keep her body safe and whole, but holding her tightly would if anything only compromise her more he knew, and tucking his hands under his knees to stop them from involuntarily reaching out to her he looked around restlessly in search of some other way to protect her. His torso rocked back and forth as he looked about uncertainly, and then unable to find what he wanted he pulled his hands out from under his knees and placed them on the earth in front of him, caressed the ground once more with his palms. He continued to caress it for some time, as if requesting the earth to help him in some way, then leaning forward slowly he began to push down into it with his palms. The ground was hard but he pressed down into it with all his weight as though to break into it, as though by reaching deep enough inside with his hands he could somehow scoop out in a single piece the section of earth on which Ganga lay, which by bearing in his arms he could use to carry Ganga to safety without having to touch her delicate body.

Dinesh stopped pushing suddenly, and raising his head gazed at Ganga's arms. They were stretched out behind her head, the right one casually bent and the left one extended out at full stretch, the hand almost at a right angle to the wrist. Not taking his eyes off this left hand Dinesh shuffled towards it on his knees and crouching down studied the long, slender fingers, which were bent slightly, though not curling or uncurling as they had when Ganga had been sleeping the night before. Wiping off his dusty hand on his sarong he hesitated for a moment, then slowly, almost fearfully, as he had done in the clearing the previous night, he clasped the tip of her thumb between his own thumb and forefinger. Lightly he caressed the hard nail and the delicate etching that formed her thumbprint, and then closing his eyes he listened in expectation. No movement. He took his thumb and forefinger to her wrist, closed his eyes and listened again, then crouching down over Ganga's head put his temple lightly against hers and waited once more in silence. Nothing happened at first, and then soundlessly a wave of muscular contraction passed from Dinesh's stomach upwards to his neck. His lips parted and his head jerked back but pulling away from Ganga as much as he could he pursed his lips firmly and did his best to stifle the movement inside his throat. He remained crouched, all his muscles tense, his forehead against the earth, and only when the wave had passed and he was sure no others were coming did his body slacken, though his eyes remained closed and he didn't move. The ground vibrated softly, almost pleasantly beneath him. A gust of warm air rushed past, stuck briefly to his moist skin before then unsticking itself. Dinesh raised his head and looked again at Ganga. He was unable to breathe in but he had stopped losing air, and as though he were still unconvinced by what his fingertips had failed to feel, he inched, slowly, without breathing, towards the center of her body. Taking care to avoid the small dark pool by her waist he reached out carefully over her stomach towards the hem of her dress and pulled it down over her knees to her shins, so that her thighs were no longer exposed. He looked her over as if to make sure that everything was in order, then tucked one hand cautiously under her left shoulder, the other under a section of her left thigh that was bloodless. Holding her as lightly as he could while still maintaining a tractable grip, since he didn't want to come too much in contact with the warmth of her flesh, he lifted the left side of her body up, carefully, from the ground, so that she lay entirely on her right side. He had wanted to roll her over onto her back slowly and gently, but as soon as he brought her center of gravity past the vertical her body tipped over of its own accord and she fell pliantly onto her back, with a soft, inaudible thud.

Ganga lay there before him, limp and silent. Her half-open eyes stared upwards in different directions, as though there was something confusing about the sky. Her right cheek, which had been pressed against the ground, was coated in dirt, the eyelid and eyebrow on that side too, and the area around her right temple was strangely bloated.

Dinesh leaned towards her face, bent down over her slowly, and brought his index finger to her left eye. As gently as he could with his fingertip, he touched the eyelid just above the lashes, and slid the thin envelope of skin down so her eye was closed. The right eye was slightly more difficult to close because of the swelling around the right temple, but he brought the eyelid down over all but a white sliver near the bottom of her eye, so that both eyes were more or less closed and her expression was less confused. With his index and middle fingers he brushed off the dirt on the right cheek, carefully but firmly. The skin remained dusty even after the dirt was brushed away, and moistening his fingertips on his tongue he dabbed a little saliva onto it, rubbing it in lightly so the cheek became a fresher shade of brown. With his index finger he stroked Ganga's left eyebrow, dusting off and straightening out all the little hairs, then he did the same for her right eyebrow, which rose up towards its edge because of the bulging around her temple. He sat back and scrutinized Ganga's face, which seemed in much better shape now, then turned towards her stomach. The section of her dress that covered it was black and wet, speckled with sand, especially glossy along a thin strip where it had apparently been ripped open, from one end of which what looked like the edge of a piece of shrapnel gave off a mute glimmer. The earth over which her stomach had lain was pasty with blood too, thick and substantial though less dark in color. Looking down Dinesh gazed at this mixture of blood and earth without moving. All of it had traveled till recently through the vessels of Ganga's body, peacefully supplying it with everything it needed for life. At some point in its progress through her arteries and veins it had even passed through the different compartments of her beating heart, but now it was being exposed to the earth and air, forced to thicken, dry, and lose its warmth.

Dinesh unbuttoned his shirt, which despite his sweat still smelled faintly of lime, then peeled it off and laid it out delicately over Ganga's stomach, so that the wound and the blood were entirely covered. He leaned back and surveyed her body, which was more presentable now, and could even have been taken for the body of someone fast asleep. As though unable still to believe that blood was no longer moving through her body, he bent down in front of her chest and put his ear to her sternum, which projected very slightly from her chest because of how her breasts slanted gently to the sides. Careful not to press too hard, in case the pressure caused blood to gush out of her stomach, Dinesh closed his eyes and did his best once more to listen.

Perhaps the heart only beat because of the blood's movement around the body, and not, in fact, the other way round. Perhaps, like a mechanism that converted kinetic energy of one kind into that of another, it was only because the living body was in perpetual motion that the blood circulated constantly inside, and perhaps the heart's only function in this process was to convert the circulation of blood into sound, into a steady, two-step beat whose sole purpose was to convey the nature of one's inner life to other living creatures, to express through its rhythm and volume the mood and feeling of its possessor to those who were close enough to hear. Dinesh sat up slowly and looked around, as though he hoped to find somewhere in the desolation an instrument by which the spilled blood could be collected, put back in Ganga's body, and set once more in motion. He looked to his left, and then to his right, then looking in front of him noticed for the first time, at the entrance to the tent, the stainless steel plate that Ganga had left inside for her father the night before. It was upside down, and scattered about it was the white rice and dhal she had made, still moist but mingled now with dirt. Her father had obviously not touched it, obviously he hadn't come back and hadn't planned to, and finding it there she had decided probably to find somebody else to give it to, or maybe to search for her father so that she could make him eat it herself. Dinesh looked for a while at the food, which if eaten now would no doubt involve biting into hard grains of sand, then turned away quietly, leaned forward onto his hands, and heaved. As if an invisible hand were reaching down into his throat and trying to pull out everything, not just air but the matter that he consisted of too, he heaved once more, and then retched, one wave following the other, heaving and retching, unable to stop. He struggled against it at first, his eyes watering and the veins along his neck and temples distending, his neck and arms tensed in an effort to prevent his body from turning itself inside out, and then, as if a switch had silently been flicked, he seemed, all of a sudden, to give in. His body slackened, he brought his head closer to the ground, and he let the waves pass without resistance along his gut and throat, as though no longer concerned with what was happening to him. He waited passively for each subsequent wave to arrive, as if willing or even wanting now to let his body be emptied, as if willing or even wanting now to let himself be lost to the atmosphere, though whether he was yielding so wholly because it was something he wanted or because it was something that would happen inevitably was difficult to say, not just difficult in fact but impossible. There were things, after all, that could happen to human beings, after which their thoughts and feelings became unknowable. There were events after which, no matter how long or intimately one has tried to be by their side, no matter how earnestly or with how much self-reproach one desires to understand their situation, how meticulously one tries to imagine and infer it from one's own experiences, one has no choice but to watch blindly from the outside. Not so much because one has not gone through similar things oneself, not so much because one lives in different circumstances, in a situation of privilege, in another part of the country or another country even, nor because one is attempting to understand from a different point of view, with a distinct vocabulary, or in another language entirely, not so much for any of these reasons which one can at least attempt to overcome but because, when such things happen to a person, the life inside them that once expressed itself on their face becomes severed from their skin, becomes lost inside their body and ceases to find expression. Like an elastic band strained too tight, like the soft waxy stem of a plant, bent, and snapped, or the thin shell of a snail, stepped on and cracked, something happens, and suddenly nothing in their actions, nothing in what they say, in the movements of their hands or legs, in their gestures or in the features of their face, nothing gives any indication of who they are or what is happening to them, so that it is impossible to guess any longer what their thoughts and feelings are, or whether they even have thoughts and feelings at all, whether there is a human being occupying their body still, or whether having diminished so much the human being has simply slipped out of their body and into the air in an otherwise unremarkable exhalation, leaving the body in some sense still alive, its hands still gripping and its feet still stepping, its bladder filling and its bowels emptying, its chest, however indiscernibly, still rising and falling, while in its gaze and expression something vital has in the meantime become absent.

Dinesh was sitting up now, his arms wrapped around his waist, his eyes glazed and out of focus. The ground beneath him was no longer quivering, and the air around him was no longer moving. Except for his hardly audible wheezing and the tight, contained spasms that his body was making, everything around him was quiet. The heavy and relentless weight of the sky had been lifted, replaced now by only a strange, weightless stillness. A gentle gust of wind blew past from the direction of the coast, where the sea continued to soundlessly advance and soundlessly recede across the sand. Dinesh leaned forward, slowly, and placed his hands on the ground in front of him. Gazing down he began to caress the soft dirt, tenderly and rhythmically, slowing to a stop, as if a thought was occurring to him, then resuming, slowing to a stop, and then resuming. All the while his chest continued to oscillate, to rise and fall independently of him, accepting and renouncing, as the atmosphere continued entering and leaving, the small volume of air that it was still able to hold.

Acknowledgments

THIS TEXT, in its present form, was made possible only by a great amount of help from a small number of individuals, none of whom I know how to thank:

My agent A.S; my editor C.B; the doctor, S.S; the writer, S.D; my advisor P.K; my friends K.B, G.K, S.K, O.N, L.P, J.R, and L.S; my sister A.A; and, most of all, my parents M.A and S.D.R.A.

About the Author

ANUK ARUDPRAGASAM is from Colombo, Sri Lanka, and is currently completing a dissertation in philosophy at Columbia University. He writes in Tamil and English. *The Story of a Brief Marriage* is his first novel.

About the Type

FOURNIER has a clean look on the page and provides good economy in text. Monotype, in 1924, based this face on types cut by Pierre Simon Fournier, circa 1742, which were called St Augustin Ordinaire in Fournier's *Manuel Typographique*. These types were a stepping stone to the more severe modern style made popular by Bodoni in the late 1700s.